Gary Nott was born in 1963. He grew up in the 1970s, reading Enid Blyton. He has been the head teacher of different primary schools for the last twenty years. Married to Suzanne, he has three young children.

Gary divides his time between school, family and writing. He loves to read his stories to his pupils. A childhood fascination with the circus sees Gary set his first novel under the big top: a tale of young love and adventure set against the debate whether to include wild animals in entertainment. Gary has also written a history textbook and a collection of assembly stories.

The Enemy Within

GARY NOTT

The Enemy Within

Vanguard Press

VANGUARD PAPERBACK

© Copyright 2015
Gary Nott

A CIP catalogue record for this title is
available from the British Library.

ISBN: 978-1-78465-046-9

*Vanguard Press is an imprint of
Pegasus Elliot Mackenzie Publishers Ltd.*

www.pegasuspublishers.com

**First Published in 2015
Vanguard Press
Sheraton House Castle Park
Cambridge England**

Printed & Bound in Great Britain

My gratitude to Suzanne, Archie, Henry and Scarlett
for their endless love.

Thanks, as always, to Mum and Dad.

For Cameron, Derek, Jasmine and James (Y6) – my
favourite audience!

And Natasha and Katherine – for all your
encouragement.

Acknowledgements

For all the circus acts I have enjoyed, but especially the bears of Circus Hoffman, and David Konyot and his steel cage entrée (Circus Harlequin).

Prologue

The tent was half empty, yet again. Laurent, the gaffer, stared up at the girl as she gracefully walked the taut tightrope. Some fourteen metres above the ring, she stared straight ahead. She had only a silver parasol to cling to, one pointed foot carefully feeling the way, then the next. She inched forward. All the while, the orchestra's drummer beat out a slow, hypnotic accompaniment. No safety harness for her – oh no, she insisted. Performers had fallen to their death before, so this was raw danger.

The crowd were busy below her, some chatting, whilst others ate. Small children were bored and fidgety but the silent majority were straining their necks ever upwards, sucking it in. They willed her on. She faltered, struggled to regain her balance (it was a choreographed stumble, not that those watching would know). It was hard to execute well, and then, steady once more, she almost ran towards the security of the platform. Applause, punctuated with whistles. The band struck up a bright tune and the house lights came up. She slid down a rope to the centre of the ring. Taking her bow, she was all smiles. Sliding back into her waiting clogs, she turned and shimmied towards the curtain. The lights went out. She was gone – out into the cold, muddy field. All glamour put away, just a woman walking, coat draped over her shoulders against the wind. She was no longer a thing of breathtaking beauty and mystery. Until that is, two hours later, when she would "live" again, at the seven thirty performance.

Laurent stayed staring at the ring for a while after. He had enjoyed watching the show, as always. The tent was empty now, more or less. There were just a few stragglers making their exit, wrapping up in coats and scarves, happy.

He was reminiscing, distant, dreamy. Thinking back thirty years to a time when the circus was packed, night after night. A time when elephants and lions had filled the ring, no human only shows then, no ban on exotic beasts! Suddenly, he was pulled up short. He was remembering the summer of '75; a wave of emotion swept over him. He had been a child then, of course, no more than twelve. He could still recall the thrill of the chase: a few weeks when he and a band of friends had to become detectives to save the circus – save it from an "enemy within".

One

1975

Four Friends

Pete wanted a girlfriend. He was eleven, going on twelve. None of his lad friends had one and he wanted to be the first in his class. He wasn't bad looking – tall with a shock of black hair. He couldn't explain why it was so important to him, it just was. Mum said he wasn't to worry because it would happen soon enough – he was only young.

He was sitting on his bed looking at the posters on his wall. Suzi Quatro was his favourite pop star, and then there was the gorgeous blonde in that new group, Abba – he fancied both stars something rotten. Of course, he had girls who were friends but they were just that, friends. There was a knock at the front door. 'It's Clive,' hollered Mum, 'I'll send him up.' There was the sound of heavy footsteps on the stairs, like an approaching baby elephant. His friend entered the room. He was a tubby boy who wore glasses, not Britain's best-looking kid – but he was kind and could be funny.

'How's things?' he asked.

'Okay,' said Pete, 'waiting for an adventure.' The two boys laughed. They were always joking that they would like an adventure, a mystery to solve like the ones they read about in books.

'Nothing doing,' said Clive. 'The only mystery we'll get is will it be maths or English first thing on Monday morning.' They chuckled. It was the weekend and the two friends liked to hang out together on a Saturday. Today, they were teaming up with Annie and Lucy from their class – just friends, mind you – no romance. They were going to the Wimpy and then in the afternoon they were set for the football match to watch Peterborough United in the last game of the season.

'I'll be a couple of minutes,' said Pete. 'Just have a quick flick with the flannel.' He disappeared off into the bathroom. *Pete was always washing*, thought Clive – *odd*. In the bathroom, posing in front of the mirror, in his cotton vest, Pete cheekily splashed on some of his dad's Brut 33; *you never know*, he thought, *I might meet that someone special this afternoon*. He came back into the bedroom, shiny and new.

'Phoorh!' said Clive, getting a whiff of the pungent aftershave. 'What exactly are you wearing?'

Pete did an impression of Henry Cooper, the boxer, who both boys often saw on TV advertising the aftershave. 'Splash it all over,' said Pete in a deep voice, mimicking the boxer's famous slogan and pretending to slap his face with cologne. Clive laughed; his friend could be such fun. 'Come on,' said Pete, pulling on a crisp, clean shirt, 'we'll be late for the girls.'

The two boys bombed down the stairs and out onto the street. 'Don't be late in,' cried Pete's mum, as the door slammed. Her words chased them the length of the street. It was warm. There was even talk of a heatwave coming that summer. They didn't know what that would feel like, never having lived through one before. Pete's mum said she could remember the winter of '63. 'If it is going to be as hot this summer as it was cold then, we are in for a treat,' she proclaimed wisely. The boys thought they knew what she meant. Pete's mum often said things that were back to front, "bum before elbow", as Clive liked to say.

The children met up outside the Wimpy Bar. The girls led the way inside to the cool and they pounced on the only vacant table, with the waitress quickly coming over. 'Someone's wearing a lot of aftershave, oh what an aroma! "Old Spice", I shouldn't fancy,' she joked. Pete blushed, the girls giggled. Clive went to correct her mistake but a frown from Pete silenced him. 'What will it be kids?' she enquired, with a cheeky grin. The children ordered four Coke floats. Whilst waiting, they chatted about their week. It had been tedious in school, as boring as a wet weekend on the seafront, for Mr Baker was focussing on their times tables. He said they must know them all, "backwards, sidewards, forwards, leftwards" – they got the idea.

'It's important,' the teacher had insisted, 'that you know them before you leave for Big School at the end of the summer.' Clive didn't know his, but the others were as bright as buttons, razor sharp in class, especially Lucy.

Big School – the children were excited, but just a little nervous too for they didn't know what to expect. Cherry Trees Primary had been their home since they were little but now everything would be different. They were, in part, trying not to think about it.

'I'm not looking forward to the move to secondary,' admitted Lucy, with hesitation in her voice.

'I don't know,' said Annie, who was the more outgoing of the two. 'Things do seem a little babyish now at Cherry Trees. I'm looking forward to making new friends. We'll do French and there's a science lab. It should be fun!' The others remained silent; they were more doubtful.

The waitress reappeared, balancing their order expertly on a tray, which she did really rather well. The kids claimed their drinks. They pushed the ice cream floating at the top of their floats deep down into the tall glasses and watched the Coca-Cola fizzle and froth. Poking their straws to the bottom, they raced each other to hoover up the delicious drink treat.

The two girls were pretty enough. Both tall, one was fair, the other dark. 'I want to buy a single before the game,' said Annie. ' "Bye, Bye Baby".' The two girls began to sing, to the tune of "This Old Man":

B-A-Y, B-A-Y,
B-A-Y, C-I-T-Y,
With an R-O-double-L, E-R-S,
Bay City Rollers are the best!
Eric, Derek, Woody too,

Alan, Leslie, we love you,
With an R-O-double-L, E-R-S,
Bay City Rollers are the best.

The boys groaned. It was embarrassing. *Were all girls in love with the Scottish Rollers that year?* It certainly seemed like it. Annie had even taken to wearing the tartan that the Rollers sported; she had a long Scottish scarf around her neck. She looked like a walking advert for the Scottish Tourist Board; all she needed was some Scottish shortbread to complete the look.

They finished their floats with a collective loud slurp, if not something approaching a raucous burp, reverberating across the restaurant. Clive then surprised the others by proceeding to ask for a burger and chips. The waitress reappeared with the order *as if my magic* – it was like something out of that cartoon show, *Mr Benn!* 'Someone's hungry,' she exclaimed. The children sat and watched him eat it. The meat juices dribbled over the toasted bun. Clive slid chutney off his knife and swallowed it in one mouthful. *The floats had been really filling, so where did he find the room for a burger?*

After they had paid the bill, they made for Woolworths, the High Street's colourful mecca, so Lucy could buy her record. It cost a sizeable 30p, but she had been saving for weeks. The children thumbed through the other singles, calling out to one another when they found something that caught their fancy. Clive wanted "Jive Talking" by the Bee Gees but he didn't have enough money. The children emptied their pockets to see if they could help, but all their pennies were needed for the match. Time was getting on and they walked down to the football stadium at a fair old pace. Having paid the entrance fee – which swallowed up the remainder of their pocket money for the week – they struggled to push their way through the extraordinarily heavy turnstiles. *Why did they have to make them like that? Were they expecting weight-lifters?*

Standing in the terraces, amongst an edgy crowd, they were all too aware that the Gulls had had a mediocre season, with a mid-table finish now certain. Fans were waving their football scarves above their head, their steadfast devotion on show. 'I've only got Tartan,' laughed Lucy, waving her scarf frantically in the air. The home team walked out on to the pitch and the four thousand or so who had gathered to watch the match drowned the stadium with a deafening cheer; it made the children's ears pop like a bag of hot Butterkist.

Someone pushed from behind. 'Careful,' said Pete shoving a glare at a small nipper who had absentmindedly toppled forward into him. His dad apologised, slapping the young boy firmly about the head. The toddler looked surprised to feel the man's hand but just managed to fight back his tears. The children forgot about it as the crowd began to chant. As the Lincoln team were announced over the tannoy, there was a resounding boo at the end of each opposition player's name. The children were enjoying themselves.

The first-half match was tight and it got progressively hotter as the afternoon wore on. At half time, the home team were up by a single goal, a slender margin that made the watching spectators nervous. Clive made his way down to the snack bar. He bought a pie and came back already scoffing it. *Really,* the children wondered, *where did he find the room?* Still, he seemed happy enough with his lot in life – he was never going to be David Essex, and he knew it. The girls were pleased because "Shang-A-Lang" by the Rollers was played at the break. There seemed no escape from the Scottish pop band, even here.

In the end, Torquay were triumphant 3–0; the children had enjoyed shouting, singing and cheering when each goal was banged home with gusto. It being the last match of the season, the players came and dutifully clapped the home fans at the end of the game. Meanwhile, there was polite applause from the crowd for the losers. With quite a crush to get out, the boys looked to make sure the girls were safe. It was the done thing – boys looked after girls – it was the 1970s – the age of chivalry was alive and kicking, thank you very much and the boys were knights in the aisles! The children walked home happy.

The next few weeks in school, came and went – sped by, if truth be told. At the weekends, there were no longer football matches to look forward to. The children were restless. Mr Baker had said there would be exams at the start of June and the children thought they had better go over some of the work they had covered that year. Pete and the girls took their revision very seriously; they had all tried for the local grammar school but only the kids of the richer parents seemed to get in. It was what Pete's mum called "looking after your own". They weren't sure what she meant – nothing unusual there. The children were instead all going to the local comprehensive.

Each of the four friends, bar Clive, enjoyed the tests: it gave them a chance to show what they could do; not showing off, mind you, just pleased to be able to say "we can do this!" Mr Baker read out everyone's position in the class results, starting with Fiona Jenkins, who came first in both English and maths – her face told its own story, smug, Pete later labelled it. In last place was Simon Jones – poor lad. Clive was second to last – "a quite shocking result", commented Mr Baker. Clive took it on the chin – not much got him down. Pete was pleased with a respectable fifth place, which would set him up nicely for the secondary school he dared to venture.

As a reward, following the tests, the children's parents treated them to an afternoon at the town's cinema. It gave them a spring in their step: who said, hard work didn't pay off? The new Disney movie was showing: *One of Our Dinosaurs Is Missing*. There was a long queue that stretched along the street, people shuffling to kill the wait. 'Will we never get in,' grumbled Lucy, who could be dreadfully impatient – she seemingly couldn't help it, but it could grate.

'Come on,' encouraged Pete. 'Let's play a game to pass the time.' Lucy reluctantly agreed, she could be grumpy as well, but she had a heart of gold and was well known for her bright ideas. They played "I Spy". Pete kept winning, although there wasn't an awful lot to spy, captive as they were in the queue; but it whiled away the time.

Then the line began to move. 'At last,' sighed the children, who had begun to think the afternoon treat would never get under way. The kids were shown to their seats by a pretty usherette. To one side of them sat a woman smoking like a chimney; she was talking loudly to her companion. 'Ssshhh,' said the usherette, who proceeded to wink at the four friends; to the other side, sat a young couple kissing. Pete looked on. He still hadn't found himself a girlfriend. Lucy and Annie were great but he didn't fancy them – they weren't his type. I mean, they liked football, which was hardly girly.

The two girls had bought a box of Maltesers, the boys a bag of Opal Fruits. They each handed them down the row and they disappeared as quickly as rabbits down a bolt-hole with a fox hot in pursuit. They enjoyed the B movie. It was the story of a dog which had lost its owner; its tale was told by a deep voiced American narrator. Laughing, the children imitated his voice, gruff with a twang. Then it was time for the main event. It was a tale of derring-do, which saw some characters looking for stolen microfilm in the Natural History Museum. During the interval, it was the girls' job to queue for Walls ice-cream tubs for all of them. At the end of the film, as they got up and turned to go, the smoking woman was still chatting ten to the dozen, the couple still kissing. The children dissolved into giggles, with the girls exchanging raised eyebrows at the sight of the young couple, who presumably had missed most of the film.

Pete still couldn't take his eyes off the two of them, so Annie gave him a firm dig in the ribs.

'Your eyes are on stalks,' she said, disapprovingly. She never missed anything, did Annie.

'Steady, tiger!' Lucy added, turning to Pete. He turned scarlet for he hadn't realised he was being so obvious. The snogging couple carried on, oblivious to the children.

The four friends strolled out of the cinema into the late afternoon sunshine, blinking at the sudden rush of light. The summer stretched out in front of them. There were only two weeks remaining of school and then it would be the start of the long, six week summer holidays. 'If only something unexpected would happen,' wished Pete. 'An adventure or mystery, like in the pictures.'

It really did seem that they were to have an uneventful time; nothing ever seemed to take place – they were just kids, after all. 'Life isn't like a Disney film,' Lucy's mum had scoffed, when asked.

As they passed a shop window, they saw a poster for a circus. It was coming to Torquay for a six week summer season. There were pictures of lions and elephants, and a clown. *Templeton's Circus,* they read, *a world of fun and amazement.* 'A circus,' commented Lucy. 'Anyone fancy it?'

Clive went to say yes but Pete jumped in with, 'Don't be silly. Circuses are for kids.' Lucy and Annie traded looks. Pete sometimes sounded like he was twenty-one!

The children moved on. In the next window, there was another circus poster, in the next, another – each one different. It did look fun. Emboldened, Clive said that he thought the show looked exciting. 'I've never seen a circus – this one has lions!'

'I saw one once,' said Pete. 'The animals were in tiny cages, it was pathetic, sad almost – they looked like they wanted to break out.'

'Don't be silly,' countered Lucy. 'I'm sure circus folk take care of their animals.' Pete shrugged his shoulders. He wasn't so sure.

Little did they know but that summer they were indeed to have an adventure; and what was even more surprising, the circus would be at the very heart of it.

Two

Arrival

The heavy lorries ran creakily over bumpy ground, like tanks on the battlefield. It was early, just past six. The morning had dawned misty, but with promise. It had already been a hot summer and today showed no sign of being anything different; it would be another scorcher – not ideal for a build-up day because the men would quickly tire. There would be much to do, as always. The breeze blew in off the sea. It was salty and so tasted distinctly different.

Olaf and Timmy were sitting high up in the cab that pulled the beast wagon. Their father, Gustav, was at the wheel. The cats had been roaring this past half hour, clearly agitated. The animals knew they would be stopping soon and they would want water. Gustav pulled the wagon over. The lorry reversed slowly into position, for they were animals on board. Then the boys' father stopped the engine. 'You boys, water the cats,' he instructed. 'I have to see the gaffer.' *He had all the life of a drowsy wasp, these days*, thought the boys.

The boys jumped down. Olaf was the older at eleven. Tall, thin, and altogether more confident than his younger brother, he had a mop of yellow hair. Timmy was shorter, tubby; you might even say "fat", especially for ten. Both looked foreign, precisely because they were Slovakian. The circus was a travelling United Nations with people coming from the four corners of the globe. The common language was German but here in the UK they tended to speak in English; it seemed only natural to do so.

The children's mother had arrived. She had been following with the caravan. She came over and ruffled Olaf's hair. 'How was the journey?' she asked. 'I lost you at the town centre.'

'Not too bad,' answered Olaf. 'Mama, I want to get my hair cut differently.'

'How?' she enquired.

'A Mohican,' he answered with a twinkle in his eye.

'Ask your father,' she replied. He groaned and turned away in abject disappointment. He knew what Dad's answer would be: "Sensible, Timmy, we must be senseebelle. We are at home with the Engleesh now. They do not like such things with their famous reserve." He said it every time, no matter the request.

They opened up the sides to the van. Behind, pacing, were majestic looking lions; just the one male but five lionesses. 'Morning, children,' said Sasha, the boys' mother. 'Sleep well?' A lioness groaned deeply at the sound of the familiar voice. The cat rubbed her face up against the bars and Sasha ruffled her cheek.

'Is the water connected yet?' asked Olaf.

'It had better be,' barked Sasha.' I am tired of waiting round for that good-for-nothing Demetrius to get his act together. I have cats. I need water.' She turned the end of the nozzle and water gushed out. 'Good,' she sighed, 'he's learning – finally!' The cats squatted to lap their water. Another day, another site; however, this one was different – not that the cats knew it. After a season of three day stands, they were to be here by the seaside for six whole weeks. This was to be home, at least for a while: Torquay, a pretty West Country town, a lovely spot that would be a holiday of sorts for the whole family. In between shows, they could go to the beach, eat outside. This glorious weather meant anything was possible.

Where was Gustav, her husband? What did he want to see the gaffer about? He was always disappearing these days. He had gone to complain, no doubt; he was always griping. He hadn't been like that when they first met. Then, he had been fresh and young, full of hope; whereas these days he was sour, bitter. If it wasn't the heat, it was the prices in the shops. He was always harping on about Slovakia as if it had all been perfect. Well she remembered, remembered why they had travelled – never enough money! At least here, with Templeton's Circus, she knew where the next meal was coming from. 'Breakfast,' she called once the barriers had been erected in front of the articulated lorry. 'Boys, breakfast!' Olaf and Timmy hurried for the caravan for they were hungry. Sausages, eggs and beans, just what the doctor ordered

(these being before the days when medics would warn against the pleasures of a fry-up!)

Food eaten, it was time to help the men build the big top. A morning of hard work for the circus hands – of mostly sitting around for the children. Build ups – the one weekday when the kids didn't have to attend the local school. The tent transporter was in position. The four king poles, giant masts, were pulled into place by a tractor. The men guided them to a vertical position. It was back breaking work and the hands were glad the sun was not yet high and at its hottest. Other workers had unloaded the tent, with the help of the circus crane. Some locals had turned out to earn a few extra pounds in their pockets, a nice little earner for those not afraid of hard work. The tent was unfurled, laid out on the ground, flat like a tailor's template for a suit that he was making for some giant or other. A gang set to hammering in the stakes that would hold the side tent poles in place. Thud, thud, thud – a rhythmic pounding rang out loudly across the ground. It punctuated the voices of the circus folk as they arrived, shouting their good mornings to one another. *Had they met traffic at the ring road? Had anyone's directions let them down?* At eleven, or thereabouts, the cry went up that signalled they were ready for the battle. This was where the children came in. Each side would now pull their part of the tent with gusto in a giant tug of war, with ropes and muscles both straining.

Job done, the children collapsed onto the grass in a fit of tired giggles.

Elsewhere, the zoo was taking shape, like a baker skilfully completing layers of a complicated cake. Templeton's Circus was home to a menagerie of wild beasts: a troupe of three Indian elephants; a string of Palomino horses; Russian bears; a giraffe aptly named George; and, not forgetting Sasha's pride and joy, the lions. The elephants had arrived and were waiting patiently in their lorry for their stable tent to be hoisted. Their trunks were poking out of the air vents on their van, as if to say, *Hello, we're here, have we been forgotten?*

However, the big top came first, always came first. Maybe it shouldn't have, but that's the way things were. The bears were pacing. The horses were tied up to the outside of their transporter, gratefully munching on fresh hay bags; their stalls would be built later. The lions could be heard roaring, deep guttural groans and moans, for they were hungry. It made Torquay sound like the African savannah. The hour was getting on and it would soon be time for lunch. The local butcher arrived with the cats' and bears' supply of meat; it was an unusual delivery but one that made him happy enough. Sasha dished the slabs out to her lions whereupon they snatched their share, squatting down in a corner of the cage to eat. The zoo was now open to the paying public and there were some punters already walking round. They were gawping at the size of the elephants; admiring the sleek coats of the horses; laughing at the antics of the bears that were play fighting comically in their cages, like amateur boxers without the gloves.

The children's mother called them. It was time to find the local supermarket and buy what they needed for the week. It was always the same routine but notwithstanding the monotony, the children enjoyed their visits to the shops. English shops were full of wonderful smelling food – the aroma was to them as sweet as nectar was to bees – and, as a treat, they knew they would be bought crisps or chocolate. It had not been like that back in Czechoslovakia where there was less colour, less variety – bland and then some! The boys didn't miss home, not one little bit.

When the children got back from shopping, tired and thirsty, the tent was all but finished. The bandstand had been pushed into place and the seats laid out. The orchestra were practising and the flyers – Kristabel, Oleg, Aaron and Pieter – were shouting out to one another from high in the rigging; they were like parrots squawking high in the trees of the rainforest. By now, the generators were busy humming but the town that was the circus was enjoying an afternoon doze in the sun, after a tiring first day.

The boys got out their work books and Mama set them some sums to do. 'Education,' she said, 'is important. You have to know what to do with words and numbers if you are to have choices in life. The circus,' she added, 'may not be for you when you are older – who can see into the future? It is important you have options!'

Laurent, their French friend, stopped by and promptly deposited himself with a self-satisfied sigh upon their caravan steps. The boys got on very well. Laurent was twelve and his parents had a tumbling act, which he joined at the weekends. His body was lithe and supple because he practised hard to keep himself fit. It was his future, he knew that.

The children were enjoying the sunshine and they had plans: when there were no shows, they would explore the beach, something each one looked forward to. Laurent was a strong swimmer, as was Olaf. Timmy didn't swim – he would be too self-conscious in trunks. It was unusual to find someone young in the show who was overweight; that state of affairs was usually reserved for the older women, when they had long since retired from the ring. Timmy wasn't bothered. His future was in showing cats. He didn't need to be able to do the things that an acrobat could. Natalie and Yolanda came running over. Strikingly pretty, they were twins, with raven black hair. The girls were just twelve, going on fifteen. The five friends were now all together. 'How's your day been?' Yolanda asked.

'Lazy this afternoon,' mumbled Timmy, suddenly feeling sweaty. 'It's been too hot to do anything much. How 'bout you?'

'The usual,' said Natalie. 'We need something exciting to happen.'

'Nothing doing,' called out Olaf, who was now lying flat on his back, his work book firmly closed. 'Nothing exciting happens round here, just work, work and just when you didn't expect it – guess what? – some more work!'

'Are you boys slacking off?' Sasha's voice floated through the open caravan window and found their target: for the boys sat up hurriedly, bolt upright.

'We've done enough for one day, can't we be excused?' chanced Olaf.

'Sounds like you already have,' countered Sasha. 'Okay, enough for one day.'

'Come on,' said Natalie. 'Let's go feed the ladies.' The children got up and ran towards the elephant tent. The intense warmth hit them as soon as they walked in, like a punch in the stomach; a veritable wall of heat. Slowly, so as not to disturb the animals, they each inched forward. The tent smelt sweetly of elephant. The children didn't wrinkle their noses, for they liked the aroma – it was "circus" – earthy, real. Inside the three enormous "ladies" were swaying musically. The beasts put their trunks out when they saw the children, as if to say, *What do you have for us?*

Bruce, the groom, was there. It was his job to clear away the dung, feed and water the creatures and get them ready for their performance. The children didn't care much for him. Sasha said he was shifty, she didn't know why the gaffer employed him. 'Bruce can't be trusted,' she confided, but she wouldn't expand to say why exactly.

The girls had some apples that they had pinched from the fruit bowl in their caravan. They would get told off for it later, but for now it felt good to have something to offer. 'Just one each,' pleaded Natalie. 'Now don't rush.' The creatures left a handful of slobber on the children's hands as they fed them. The kids wiped their hands on their trousers without a second thought; elephant slime didn't bother them, nothing did. The small treats were gone in seconds.

The grey, dry elephants had continued to sway all the while. Rebecca, the matriarch, sneezed on some straw. The children burst out laughing. The noise from the elephant was deafening. 'At least, it wasn't a fart,' said Timmy. The children laughed again. They knew what the elephants could do with their bottoms – clear the tent with a single waft, and then some!

'I wonder what school will be like tomorrow?' pondered Laurent. 'Difficile, sans doute, des questions et après ça, encore!' The children nodded. The first day at any new school was always full of questions – *What was it like to live in a circus? Were the animals well cared for? What did they do in the show?* That was from the children, and as for the teachers, well they would have questions of their own. *What had they done in the last school? What did they know? Could they read?*

That night they all found it difficult to sleep. The caravans were hot, stifling like blazing ovens from which there was no escape. True, the windows were all open, but it didn't seem to help as there was no breeze, despite their spot by the sea. One of the lions roared, another answered. The children each lay there, tossing and turning, thinking that the next six weeks would go as they had planned. They were looking forward to them: sunshine, seaside, and no moving on. Yes, the weeks would be as they planned them. Little did they know that they were to be anything but – Templeton's Circus was about to be struck by mystery and adventure…

Three

School

The five circus friends, relaxed and in good spirits, gathered around the twins' caravan. They always met there. It was a routine, their routine. They set off in shorts and T-shirts, brown from weeks spent outdoors. The school was a stone's throw away. It had large black gates and a pretty sign: *Cherry Trees Primary School – Please Report to Reception.*

The children did as the sign said for they knew the drill. They spoke to the flustered secretary, who spoke to the head teacher, who in turn spoke to the teachers. *Circus children, travellers, in town for six weeks. Some far too big to be Upper Juniors but were saying that's what they were. Who did they think they were fooling? Trouble with a capital "T". What were the staff meant to do with them?* The teachers scratched their heads – not what they wanted, not at all. They would only stir the other kids up, get them restless, over excited, and in this heat too. The school building was oppressively airless and stuffy. Whilst outside at playtime the schoolchildren just milled around like camels seeking shade at an oasis; the playground water fountain was endlessly popular. There were only two weeks to go till the end of term, for goodness sake. Was it even worth these circus kids coming at all? *And what would they be able to do? Not much*, the teachers imagined. They would be baby-minding them, nothing more.

The five children stood out like nobody's business. For a start, all the other kids were in uniform – shirts and ties. The school kids stood and stared at them. They were unusual and completely unexpected; in their own way, as exotic as the animals in their show. It was the first time a circus had visited their town for many years but the school kids knew it had been coming for the posters had been everywhere, but they had never imagined circus children would descend upon their school. And then the questions began. *How old are you? What do you do in the show? Why aren't you in uniform? How long are you staying?*

At break time, the other kids had crowded around them. By lunch-time, novelty gone, the circus friends were on their own – isolated, shunned – for they were outsiders. Lessons were interesting, for them at least. The teachers assumed they could do nothing, couldn't read or do maths. But all five were bright. Their parents wanted them to do well at school. They worked hard outside of school too. It wasn't easy, always on the move, but they managed to do what a lot of kids in the class couldn't. It didn't endear them to the watching children of Torquay.

That night, the circus kids gathered around the steps of the caravan after the five o'clock show. They were chatting about their day. They felt uneasy, edgy. They were tired of not fitting in, of being the odd ones out. How would they get through the next two weeks at the same school? They were used to much shorter stays. The school kids weren't exactly friendly. Maybe they should try talking to them tomorrow, make friends, maybe invite some to the show. Timmy wasn't so sure. 'Forget them, they're a bunch of losers. We're different,' he argued, 'not like them. We don't mix, don't belong.' Despite Timmy's misgivings, they decided that they would give it a try. Timmy had been outvoted so he sulked; it was what he did.

The morning dawned already warm. Laurent and the others were determined to be friendly with some of the school kids. They threw a few shapes, rolled a few back-flips. It was as easy as a butcher slicing bacon in his shop. They chatted about the lions and elephants. It worked. By the end of the day, they had made pals – Clive, Annie, Pete and Lucy – they had all been friendly to them. Clive was stocky, like Timmy. Annie and Lucy were confident girls, Upper Junior prefects, going into Secondary Y1 next year. Pete was a laugh. In fact, they were all great, really interested in their new "circus friends" and what they had to say. The boys had played football, whilst the girls chatted. 'Would you like to visit us at the show?' the five had asked. 'Circus?'

At nearly twelve, they were already feeling a bit too old for the circus. But they were intrigued. There was something about these kids, something raw, like sugar cane and different, oh so different. 'Sure thing,' came the reply. Even from Pete, the grown-up one.

'Absolutely,' he replied, 'haven't been to one for years, should be a laugh.' The circus kids walked back to the site, happy and cocksure. They had made friends with the local kids. Things were looking up, new faces, new stories to share. This summer was beginning to feel just a little different. They were here for six weeks – it was a lifetime.

At the gate, stood a group of "cranks", the word the circus folk gave to protesters against the use of wild animals in circuses. They were a large group, numbering around twenty people. They seemed to be led by a tall, authoritative figure who a crank addressed as Dave. He wore a bright red T-shirt that declared *All meat is murder!* 'Have protest, will travel,' commented Laurent. The others didn't know what he meant exactly, but it sounded rather good. The protesters were handing out leaflets and they were talking to drivers as cars pulled into the car park, trying to persuade the punters to turn round; the protesters wanted the public to take their money elsewhere.

To the circus children, the assembled gang looked angry and aggressive, like they were spoiling for a fight. As the children pushed past them, one of the antis, the cranks, spat at them. *To think, who would spit at children?* Olaf spat back, like a rasher sizzling in a pan.

'Don't get involved,' protested Natalie, in a firm voice.

'Why not?' retorted Laurent, who copied Olaf and cheekily showed them two fingers. 'Who do they think they are?'

The protesters had placards and signs that declared: *The circus is no fun for the animals!* and *Animals out, people in!* There were pictures of tigers behind bars and elephants in tutus. The ringleader, this Dave fellow, had a loudhailer that invited passing motorists to "honk" if they were against the circus. Some did, whilst others didn't. It made most of the children feel uncomfortable. All except Natalie, who harboured a secret; it was a deep secret at that, one she guarded closely. Privately, Natalie agreed with the protesters although she would never let on, of course, for her life wouldn't then be worth living. Animals were part of their show. The circus folk were united against the cranks, whom they saw as a threat to their way of life. But, Natalie thought that there was no place for animals in a modern circus. This was 1975 after all, times had changed. She liked to think that the circus could survive without the beasts – animals should be free in their natural habitats and not chained or caged. She kept quiet. She felt like a traitor – someone who was against her own family and friends. Circus for her meant something else; that didn't mean it had to be something that was worth less, did it? One day, things might be different.

Next day at school, all the class were talking about the protesters they had seen at the circus gate. How did the circus folk feel about them, camped on their doorstep? Weren't they intimidating, loud, hateful even? The teachers chatted through the two sides of the argument with the children but they were careful to do it sensitively, carefully – emotions could run high when animal cruelty was explored. The Y4 children were quick to take sides in the debate. Were their friends for, or against, animals in the circus? The subject was made real by the presence of the "Templeton" children. This was interesting – it was a true-life drama.

The teachers decided to play "conscience alley". Children were to stand on either side of a child who would walk through the alley. On one side, would be a group of children arguing for animals in the circus. On the other side classmates would argue against. It was compelling. Children were getting excited, stating their case strongly, passionately.

Pete was chosen to walk through the alley. What would he decide at the end of his walk? *'Animals should not be in the circus,'* was his answer. *'It is cruel.'* There were shouts of derision from the opposing side; kids were hyped up, spoiling for a fight; the teachers were just about containing them.

Next came Annie, who voted "for". She thought circus folk treated their animals well, kindly. They all enjoyed the lesson because it was different. All, that is, save Timmy and Olaf. They were a family who owned "cats". The debate was too close to home for them. They didn't like people shouting them down. Animals, for them, would always have a place under the big top; it was their history, their life – it would never change.

After tea, their friends from school arrived at the campsite. The five ribbed Pete about what he had said about animals in the circus. They joked around, teasing one another. The girls grouped together, linked arms.

The boys shoved and pushed one another, all in good fun – they were fast becoming "mates". 'Come and meet our animals,' the twins implored, not that the school children needed any persuading. The circus kids took them to see the lions, elephants and finally the bears; the circus children were like a magician pulling rabbits proudly out of his hat. Each of the animals was impressive in their own right but taken together they were a truly awesome collection: a Noah's ark.

'But they are all chained up,' Pete observed, starting again, 'or caged. That can't be right, surely?'

'Look at how well we keep them,' countered Timmy, irritated. 'Look into their eyes, they are bright and curious. They are part of our family, why my mum even calls them her children. Look at their coats, see how they shine.' Pete wasn't so sure; he saw boredom in the animals' stares but didn't want to upset his new friends, so he decided to keep schtum, just shrugged his shoulders by way of protest. Natalie stayed quiet too, she liked Pete. She would even go so far as to say that she fancied him. He was different to the circus boys, definitely not what she was used to.

It was Friday and they had been in Torquay for just five days. The five had become nine and were content with their new friendships. The circus children had invited their school pals to come to the five o'clock show on Saturday. It was always busy, packed even. The circus was popular, an established treat for all the family! The ringmaster, their friend, Tom Parker, had promised to "show the kids in". This was the circus way of saying they would be guests, wouldn't have to pay. Tom was a commanding figure. He was tall and handsome with a crisp moustache; he had huge hands, banana fingers, and looked as if the coat hanger remained in his jacket, so stiff was he. He never went anywhere without his whip and riding breeches. The four school friends were excited – this would be fun. They had enjoyed making friends with the circus kids who were different, interesting, and yes, exotic even. They were looking forward to Saturday – big time!

Four

The Show

The queue for the five o'clock show stretched all the way back into the car park like a pack of dominoes stood to attention. The circus was popular and wild animals undoubtedly made them so.

The four school friends were dropped off by Clive's dad. They didn't need an adult to accompany them to the show. They were, after all, eleven, going on twelve. There was no "stranger, danger" – children ran free, played outside and went places on their own. They would be allowed to make their own way home to be in before nine.

Their circus pals were there to greet them at the booking office, all except Laurent, who was performing and Timmy, whose turn it was to help get the cats ready for the show. 'Are you sure we don't have to pay?' asked Lucy, feeling just a little awkward.

'You are our guests,' replied Olaf, with a vigorous nod. 'Just follow us – stay close.'

At the entrance to the big top, stood some people dressed in colourful costumes, red coats with gold buttons; they wore bright make-up, which was literally caked on. It made them seem larger than life. A tall girl smiled at them.

'They're being passed in,' said Natalie. 'Tom has agreed.' The children went beneath the heavy underside of the tent. The day had been hot and things were sticky in the big top. Not that the children noticed, for their eyes were swept along with the explosion of colour and noise that bombarded their senses. It seemed different to when they had been younger. They were more conscious of the show people, who seemed so different to what they were accustomed. There was a buzz of excitement, excited chatter all around them. People were taking their seats, buying candyfloss, ice creams or programmes.

'Zis way,' chirped the tall girl like a sparrow but with a foreign accent, and she strode off to the right, in her thigh-high shiny black boots, a quick click of the heels echoing in the children's ears. The circus ring sat centre stage. The sawdust was sparkling under the lights that shone down upon it. The beams of light that descended showed up all the dancing dust in the air. In the ring was sitting a steel cage, the walls of which stood far higher than the children. There was a net draped over the top, suspended from a hook hanging high up in the centre of the big top.

Lions, thought Clive. 'It must be the first act,' he cried, with a burst of excitement; he couldn't help himself. He felt silly afterwards, for the others were looking at him like he was just a little kid. The children gingerly stepped over guy ropes that were strewn across their path. They were to sit ringside – in the most expensive seats. Tom Parker had seen to it for he was a good friend to the circus kids. The seven children took their places. The four school children could not help but be excited and they all felt grown up, out for an evening without their parents.

'I'd like to buy a programme,' ventured Pete. The programmes were 10p. He had 5p, but the girl selling them said just to give her what he had. The school pals poured over the programme. It was a mixture of information and adverts, interlaced with photos of the acts that they could expect to see that very evening. Every act looked shiny, star spangled and seemed to jump out of the pages. Lucy and Clive strained to look at the programme, which Pete was guarding jealously in his lap. Elsewhere, two men were passing through the crowd. They seemed to be stopping at intervals and there was the flash of an instant camera. 'What's that all about?' asked Pete, intrigued.

'You can have your photo taken with one of our lion cubs,' said Olaf. 'Do you fancy it?' Pete wasn't so sure, but Clive thought it sounded fun. Olaf beckoned the men over. One of them had a lion cub in his arms.

'You want cute photo?' asked the man, who was tall and tight-lipped.

'No photo,' instructed Olaf. 'It's expensive,' he explained over his shoulder, 'but let my friend hold the cub.' The man shrugged impatiently, but did as he was beckoned. Olaf was the lion boss' son. The cub playfully bit on the boy's trouser leg, not hard, just with baby or cub teeth.

'Wow,' said Clive as the offspring was lifted safely back. 'That was amazing.'

'We have three cubs,' said Olaf. 'They belong to my parents, not to Mr Templeton.' The school children detected a distinct hint of pride in his voice.

The children suddenly became conscious of some men climbing up into the bandstand, which stood over the entrance to the ring. By looking closely, Pete realised that this bandstand was itself a lorry; he could see the number plate at one end: a lorry that unfolded its sides and roof to make a bright show front that had an entrance from which hung floor-length, red, luxurious curtains. It was from there that the acts would emerge, one by one. It really was too exciting for words. 'It says the elephants are first,' said Clive, 'but they can't be because the ring cage is up.'

'The order of the programme changes,' said Olaf. 'The cats are always first or last. If they were last in the show before, they will be first now – that way we can leave the ring cage set up.' Clive thought he understood and Pete nodded; it made sense, less work to do.

'Is it about to start?' enquired Clive. The circus pals didn't have time to respond for all of a sudden there was a loud blast on a whistle. It was show time! The band struck up a bright tune and the ring curtains were swept back. The lights went up and performers spilled on to the ring wall, marching, clapping in time to the music. They stopped to face the audience, hands above their heads, feet stomping, encouraging the crowd to clap along. The school friends joined in. This was fun. In the middle of the performers, at the front of the ring wall, centre stage with a spotlight on him, stood Tom Parker, the ringmaster, resplendent in red-tail coat, white breeches, black boots and a shiny black top hat.

'Ladies and gentlemen, boys and girls, welcome to Templeton's Circus!' The packed crowd burst into applause and some stamped their feet. The noise was deafening, the atmosphere electric.

The performers marched off to the claps of the spectators, all smiles, waving back over their shoulders as they left the ring.

A second whistle blew. The lights went out. The big top was plunged into darkness. There was an "ooh" from the crowd.

Then a single spotlight came on. It pointed into the centre of the ring where there had appeared, as if by magic, a clown sitting on a stool. He was putting on his make-up, looking all the while into a small mirror that he held in his hand. 'He's putting on his slap,' whispered Yolanda, 'his make-up,' she added by way of an explanation.

'It's Chaos, our clown,' added Natalie. Suddenly the spotlight shone away from the clown to a nearby lion's stool, one of six positioned around the inside of the cage. Sat on top of it was a cuddly toy lion. A spotlight lit up Chaos' face, he pretended to look frightened. The crowd laughed. Chaos ran from the cage taking the toy with him, careful to shut the cage door after him. Then there was another blast of a whistle. White lights went up on the ring. The band struck up a fast tune and into the ring cage from a tunnel opposite ran a lioness with loose limbs. She stopped, blinked at the crowd and having walked slowly to her stool, jumped onto it in one bound. She opened her mouth into a large yawn, saliva dripped down from her teeth, and she squatted down into position. With no warning, a second lioness came bounding down the tunnel into the ring, then a third, then a fourth and a fifth. The crowd gasped. A murmur of appreciation rippled amongst them. They were in the presence of something quite beautiful, and they knew it.

Finally, a lion with full mane came prancing in, he stood and stretched out, feet forward, his back arched, full length, as if to say, *I'm here, we can begin now!* A lioness sitting near to the children stood and lifted her tail. She squirted scent at the neighbouring seats. Unpleasant but nevertheless spectacular! She seemed to be saying to the watching children, *Who do you think you are?*

With a clatter and shout, the lion tamer opened the ring cage door and entered. It was Gustav, decked out in a white safari suit, together with pith helmet and whip. He looked like something out of a Tarzan movie. The next five minutes seemed liked an age. It was scary stuff. The school children sat on the edge of their seats. The lions snarled and snatched, threatening their trainer. The circus children sat unmoved. They knew it was all an act, pretence. The lions had been schooled to be edgy, to appear difficult. They weren't *tame*, but they were *trained*. There were two ways of showing cats: à la douceur, where the trainer made them look like tabby house pets;

alternatively, they could be showed à la ferocité, where they would growl and snarl. These cats were shown just like that. They swiped at Gustav whenever he came close by, and he stared them down. He banged his whip and stick together loudly in a brash act of defiance.

As quickly as it had started, it was over and high above the ring the spotlight found a vision in white silk and leotard: Elena who twisted her body over, in turn after turn, hanging from the rope by just one hand looped through. The music had changed. It was now slow and pulsating and the crowd chanted out the number of times that Elena could flip her body right over.

There was a loud thunder of applause. Clive thought he had never seen a woman as beautiful as she. He had sat mesmerised. 'A penny for them,' smirked Pete.

The ring was suddenly filled with noise and laughter. It was Chaos and friends. They proceeded to cause havoc. They drenched each other with water and foam. The crowd, including the children, were soaked as a clown's bucket of slosh came in their direction; shoulders sat up as people felt the cold water hit their bodies. There was general mayhem. Chaos ended up with shaving foam all over his face. The children noticed that he was quite particular to keep it out of his flowing yellow hair. *Odd*, they thought.

Then the mood changed. "Big Band", jazzy music filled the air, saxophones and a lead clarinet. The six Arabian stallions came cantering into the ring. They did a clever routine, chopping and changing direction, all in time to the music (although truth be told, it was the band who were keeping time to the horses rather than the other way around). The act finished with one of the stallions doing a hind leg walk. The crowd showed their appreciation. Then another stallion was brought forward to bow. It was a laboured move; the trainer had to insist three times that the horse would do it, would concede and lower his body, one foot outstretched. The horse didn't seem to want to. Pete felt uncomfortable, as did Natalie but, finally, the animal obliged and the crowd clapped hard.

The lights came up. It was the interval.

'Wow!' said Lucy. 'That was brilliant, fabulous. Really!'

'I'm glad you enjoyed it,' beamed Natalie.

There was a raffle. 'Buy a ticket,' prompted Olaf. 'You'll win. Trust me.' Lucy didn't see how he could say that. But she bought some tickets. Tom Parker strode into the middle of the ring. He asked for a volunteer to pick a ticket. He chose Olaf to pick it.

'And what is the number?' queried Tom into his microphone.

'Eighty-three,' Olaf replied, looking at the ticket that he stood holding in his hand. It was one of Lucy's. She collected her prize, a cuddly lion like the one they had seen Chaos with at the top of the show. 'I said you would win,' laughed Olaf, showing her the ticket he had pulled out of the hat. It was number nineteen. He gave Lucy a grin. Lucy all at once felt like a ventriloquist's dummy, stiff and wooden. She felt embarrassed for she realised that she hadn't won fairly. Olaf had cheated, but he seemed very pleased with his trick. Tom Parker winked at Lucy, who blushed.

Ice cream! The children all had one. They told each other about their favourite bits. For Lucy, it was the lions, but Clive was still thinking about Elena.

The second half came and went.

Laurent appeared in his parents' act. They twisted into shapes and supported each other, balancing off the ground. The strength that he displayed was immense. At times, their faces went red and their muscles bulged with the effort of holding each other balanced off the ground. Laurent nodded towards them and shot his friends a thumbs-up at the end of the routine.

The highlight was undoubtedly the three *ladies* – Inga, Riga and. Flossie. The elephants lumbered into the ring, and stood large, towering over the people sat ringside. Sawdust shot up and there was a pungent whiff of elephant. The children literally had their breath taken away. Manu, who showed them, used nothing but his voice to command the elephants – no whip, no stick. At one point, he even left the ring to sit in the stands and shouted out his commands from there. It was an impressive feat. Clive was happy that there was no whip involved. It wouldn't have seemed right to use one on such magnificent beasts. Pete couldn't help but wonder what had been done to the elephants away from the audience's gaze to make them so obedient. Had they been bullied? The three pachyderms rose to put their feet on each other's backs in a hind leg stand, and then sat up on their bottoms to face the audience. *The elephants did seem relaxed*, thought Pete. He watched as they blew sawdust up on to their backs whilst they stood waiting in the wings for their turn to enter the ring to perform a special trick.

The final act was a "jockey act" involving the laughing crowd. A horse was led in. Members of the audience were invited to step forward to try to tackle the "unrideable horse" for a £1 prize plus a free truss, whatever that was! 'He can't be ridden,' claimed Tom Parker loudly. 'He's not broken in.' As each member of the audience stepped forward they tried to ride the animal, but didn't succeed. They slipped and struggled to stay on, all falling into the guiding arms of a circus groom running alongside the horse. Until, eventually, someone climbed on board and didn't realise that a safety harness had been coupled to his belt. As the horse flew round the ring, some circus hands pulled on the harness rope, which was stretched over a pulley high in the big top, and the rider was catapulted into the air and went sailing round the ring, his legs flaying about. The punter was suspended high in the tent and the audience laughed, they were in stitches.

After an hour and a half of fun, spills and excitement, the end came all too quickly. Tom Parker bade the crowd farewell and the crowd clapped their appreciation with enthusiasm. The school pals whooped loudly. Their circus friends' eyes shone. They were happy to see that their new friends had enjoyed themselves. The audience could see the animals in the zoo afterwards for 10p. All the money, they were told, would go towards the creatures' keep; with that said, it seemed almost impolite not to join the people milling through the artistes' entrance out into the evening sunshine to see the animals in their sleeping quarters. The school children made their way out, but not before their entrance fee was waived. They were happy. They had enjoyed the show and had been made to feel "treated" – special, important!

Thankfully, it was much cooler outside than it had been in the tent. The cats were lounging in their lorry. They had just been fed and were basking in all their glory as the crowds gathered round.

The three "ladies" were swaying in their tent. They were pulling at the chains round their legs. Pete couldn't help but think it would be nice for them to be able to move about freely. Natalie seemed to know what he was thinking. She frowned, but said nothing. The horses were busy munching in their stables.

Templeton's Circus was a success. People flocked to see it.

The children had made plans. On Monday they would go to the beach after school. There were no shows on the first weekday. Nothing but good times seemingly lay ahead – new friends, new experiences. They were now firm friends. Nothing could upset their happiness. Little did they know, intrigue was lurking just around the corner...

Five

An Evening at the Beach

The school day dragged by interminably. The nine friends were impatiently looking forward to an evening at the beach. They were to take a picnic that Natalie, Annie and Lucy had organised; there were to be egg sandwiches and sausage rolls. Clive and Timmy were especially looking forward to it: *food, glorious food*!

Despite his best intentions, Mr Baker was growing a little tired of the circus children. The five travellers had a lot to say for themselves, boundless confidence and clearly no self-esteem issues to worry about. The teacher registered his irritation with low mutters under his breath – not at all typical of the man. Truth be told, everyone in school was tired, for it had been a long year and there was only the one week of the summer term left; they felt like seasoned hill climbers who had a mountain's summit now firmly within their sights.

On Friday night, there would be the long awaited end of year disco organised by the Parent Teachers' Association. It would be an opportunity to get up close and personal with a girl during the dancing. Some boys were *particularly* looking forward to it, whereas some girls were a little less sure. Finally, the school bell indicated the end of a long school day. The children erupted into the playground with shouts and whistles, and the nine friends joined up with one another gleefully. They made for the gate and headed directly for the seafront. 'Where shall we settle?' asked Laurent, the children being washed along by their obvious excitement.

'How about a walk down the pier?' suggested Natalie. They all thought this a good idea. The pier was a long walk and they began to strip off as they went, for under their clothes, the children were already wearing bathing costumes. At the end of the pier were some cocky teenagers who were fishing. The children sneaked a peek into the lads' buckets to see what they had caught. There was a large fish in one of the pails, indicating one of the boys had been lucky!

Clive was struggling with his trunks. They were clearly too big for him. His mum had not found it easy to buy something right for him and had settled for the next size up. He pulled them up with one hand and groped his day clothes and bag with the other.

The children started to push one another in fun. *Who would be first to jump off the pier into the water?* Laurent dived in spectacular fashion. He was strong and lithe. Natalie jumped and then Pete. Timmy, the non-swimmer of the group stood to one side to watch; he felt awkward just standing there but he didn't swim, it was no more complicated than that.

Last to go was Clive, pulling his trunks up, much to the amusement of the others. He jumped. He went down deep into the water and then shot up to the surface in a foamy rush of water. He blinked, rubbing the water out of his eyes. *What was that bobbing in front of him?* His heart skipped a beat. He recognised the bundle of material – it was his shorts. He felt down in the water. He was naked; his shorts had come off. He turned round, simultaneously straining to keep his head aloft and one eye on the trunks, which were now moving quickly through the water. Clive realised that one of the boys fishing had "caught" his swimwear. Even now, they were reeling the trunks up to where they were standing on the pier. The group of lads were laughing, pointing to the unusual catch. Lucy looked at Clive and could see his embarrassment. In a flash, she realised what had happened. 'Tell me they're not your trunks,' she said. She couldn't help but shriek with laughter. Clive was splashing at the surface with his hands, trying to ensure that none of the children could see down to his "bits".

Only Natalie didn't laugh. She called out to the boy who was pulling his rod into his body for the sodden trunks were already weighing his line down. 'Throw them back, you've had your laugh,' she chided.

Laurent realised between his laughter that Clive was dying with embarrassment. 'If you don't throw them back, I'll come out and take them back, and you with them,' he threatened, his blood now boiling under the cold water. Laurent was muscular above the waves and looked to the lads who were fishing like he could easily handle himself.

'All right,' said the lad on the pier, 'don't get over excited, keep your trunks on!' At this remark, his watching friends burst into more laughter. The boy unhooked the pants and threw them to Laurent, who caught them effortlessly and proceeded to lob them towards Clive, who flung his arms out and grabbed them gratefully. His ordeal wasn't quite over for the tubby boy then struggled to pull them on under the water.

'Come on,' said Natalie, 'give him a break, we've had our laugh now.'

The children splashed about some more and then swam towards the beach. They ran into the warm sunshine and the boys went to fetch their bags from the pier end. When they came back, the children laid out their towels and opened up the basket with the picnic things inside. They handed round the treats and fell back onto the towels like cascading dominoes. The swim had made them ravenous.

Lying back in the sun, they all closed their eyes. Their chatter grew increasingly louder. 'What makes a circus special?' asked Clive, day dreamingly.

'You need three things,' said Laurent; he had heard the gaffer repeat it many times. 'You need ohhs, ahhhs, and ughhhs!' The school children chortled.

'What do you mean exactly?' said Pete, bemused.

'When the lions came into the ring, what was the first thing the crowd did?' asked Natalie.

'They went "ohh", replied Pete, getting it.

'And the ahhhs?' mused Lucy, hot under the baking sun.

'The "ahhs" came when you saw Elena high up on the slack rope,' replied Natalie. 'Clive can still remember it, can't you, Clive?' she added. Clive, who went red, was pleased the others couldn't see his embarrassment with their eyes closed. Since the show, the young boy couldn't talk about Elena without getting tongue tied. 'And finally, there's the "ughhh"!' said Natalie. 'You all said it when Laurent's dad bent his strained body over backwards and his muscles looked like they were going to pop out of his skin. Ohh, ahhs and ughhs, a good circus needs all three.'

They played a game of handball afterwards: the school kids, plus Laurent, versus the remainder of the circus kids. The latter were quicker with their reactions, even Timmy, and they won, even though they were outnumbered.

Time was getting on. The red sun had begun to lower in the sky and it was getting a little cooler. 'Time we were getting back,' said Laurent. 'Let's get changed.' The girls went to one side, the boys to the other. Laurent and Pete secretly glanced in the girls' direction. Natalie and Yolanda were pretty and were developing fast into young women. Both boys fancied Natalie, who glanced in their direction. Both boys' stares hit the sand; they went as red as the lobsters that were for sale along the seafront. Natalie smiled and Yolanda, catching her sister's nod in the boys' direction, burst out laughing. Laurent wasn't amused. His mood changed and he suddenly looked sulky. Now changed, Natalie went and ruffled his hair and he ran after her. He wanted to catch her. *Would she always be too quick for him?*

They were soon all dressed, with the girls' wet hair tied back. As they made their way over the sand, the ground shifted lazily beneath their feet and the school kids fought to keep their balance. Having climbed to the top of the steps, they walked out onto the promenade. The girls stopped to put their flip-flops on, rubbing the sand from their feet. Ouch, the ground was still hot; it had been baking in the sun nicely all afternoon, thank-you-very-much.

They crossed over the road and began to walk along the row of shops, in the direction of the circus site. As they made their way down the street, they glanced in the windows. Then the children saw it. One by one, they stopped in their tracks, nothing short of incredulous. There was a large poster for the circus in one of the windows and slapped bang across the middle of it was a large *VISIT CANCELLED* banner. Going into the next shop, the same *VISIT CANCELL*ED sign leapt out at them. It was a similar story all along the street. Cancelled? The circus' stay couldn't be cancelled, could it? What exactly was going on?

Six

Suspects

They dashed back to the ground. Outside the booking office, stood Tom Parker and the gaffer, with Sasha and Gustav and a crowd of other performers – all were deep in conversation. Tom looked up when he saw the children, his eyebrows knitted together in a heavy frown.

'No, before you ask, we haven't cancelled the stand. Someone has been up to dirty tricks.' The normally oh-so jovial ringmaster clearly had anger to vent; all the children could tell. 'The shopkeepers say they were visited by a man earlier today who said he was from the show. The blighter said the circus was moving on. It was he who stuck up the "Cancelled" signs.' Tom's voice dropped to a low whisper. 'The interesting thing was, that he knew lots of things about us, things that only we circus people would know: who the gaffer was and even what the next town was.' (Something the circus folks never shared with outsiders.)

The news instantly made the circus children bothered, and hotter still. Who would do such a thing? This would undoubtedly mean trouble for the show. People wouldn't come. Worse still, the circus performers would not get paid. Weeks of work went into preparing any show's visit to a town. The circus relied upon the oxygen of publicity, with posters to draw the crowds in. What would the gaffer do? What could be done? Already Torquay's families would be making other plans, with their children disappointed that the hotly anticipated treat had been spoilt. It was serious. Children and animals needed to be fed. The circus families didn't have savings. They lived from hand-to-mouth, it was their way.

What to do?

The gaffer called a staff meeting in the tent for seven thirty. The school kids made their way home, mindful of the fact that it was a disappointing end to their day. They felt that the circus folk wouldn't want them around; they were outsiders and tempers were clearly frayed.

The circus children crept into the tent and sat quietly at the back. The atmosphere was tense; the adults were seriously uptight. Some were saying that the show might as well move on. However, the next ground was not booked for another four or five weeks, not before September – it was an age. They couldn't just pack up and pull onto another ground somewhere else. It didn't work like that. Things had to be arranged, planned for. To arrive in a town with no warning never went down well with the terribly touchy authorities. The circus had to be careful that they didn't get on the wrong side of important people who could block the show coming back in future years; it would be cutting off your nose to spite your face.

The gaffer used the microphone to address them. They fell quiet. 'It might have been the cranks,' he offered, 'looking for trouble – like they always do.'

'But,' interjected Gustav, 'how did the man, whoever he was, know where we are headed next?' The circus folk nodded in enthusiastic unison; like toy dogs that could be spied in the back of a Ford Capri! Circus folk didn't share this kind of information with outsiders – they knew the kind of trouble the cranks could cause if they knew there was a show due in town: they would rip down posters, write to the press, stir up a hornet's nest. The gaffer didn't say it, but they were all thinking the same thing. Could it have been one of their own? Somebody on the inside? The children looked around the tent – everybody was there. Lots of them looking awkward, shuffling from one foot to another. A cloud of suspicion hung in the air. It was oppressive. Why would anyone have wanted to cause trouble for such a decent, hard-working show?

The bad-tempered meeting broke up with more grumbles and moans, borne out of worry more than anything else. It had been decided that the advance crew, who had been laid off for the summer season, would be contacted. These men would set to work in the coming days, visiting shops with new posters and banners that declared, *Torquay's wonder show. We're still here!* It would take a little while to get the slogans printed, and the cost would have to come out of their wages, but what other choice was there?

The next day, the show was practically empty. Word had got about that the circus had moved on and only a handful of punters, still not seemingly in the know, had turned up. The atmosphere was as dead as a Torquay weekend in November. The circus folk fed off their audience, without their reaction – the ohhs, ahhs and ughhs – the whole thing fell flat. It was bitterly disappointing for Templeton's Circus. The gaffer sent word that Wednesday and Thursday's shows would be cancelled. The news shocked the performers to the core. Cancel a show, it was unheard of. He said that they would re-open at the weekend, once the new posters and banners were in shop fronts. The circus folk were not pleased. No shows meant no wages. They grumbled but there was nothing that they could do – he was the gaffer, what he said went.

That morning on the way to school the children walked without talking. After all, what was there to say? Their parents were fed up and the mood was infectious. A gloom had descended on the show; it was difficult to see daylight. Their school pals gathered round them in the playground, like bees round a honeypot. They wanted news. What was the latest? Would they be moving on? No, came the reply, but it had been touch and go. The gaffer had decided to fight back against whoever it was. The circus children were glum. Their school pals tried to cheer them up, but there was nothing doing. They could barely raise a smile, not even with talk of the Friday night disco. They were still coming, weren't they? 'Maybe, we'll see,' came a non-committal response.

The school pals were disappointed, for they had wanted to show off their new friends – of whom they were proud. The circus kids were so different, yet they had accepted them into their world, letting them have a glimpse of what was happening behind the curtains. Pete was disappointed too. He had not been able to think of anything but Natalie in the past few days. He was smitten and had been thinking he would get to dance with her at the disco – maybe, afterwards, even sneak a kiss.

'Look,' said Pete, desperate to head off any disappointment with Natalie, 'how 'bout we get our thinking caps on?' It was his mum's favourite phrase when they were stuck for what to do. 'Who are the suspects? Let's try and work this out. If someone's got a grudge against the show, who might it be?'

'A crank,' suggested Laurent.

'Yeh,' said Timmy. 'That geezer called Dave – him with the loudhailer – he spat at me, remember?'

'Yes, he was stirring the punters up good and proper at the gate,' added Yolanda.

'But how would he have known where we were headed next? Remember, that's what the shopkeepers said about him. He knew that, this bloke,' said Natalie.

'The enemy!' spat Laurent. 'That's what we should call him. Only one of our own would know such a thing.'

So who at the circus would have done such a thing? The children thought.

Olaf looked up. 'There's Bruce, the elephant groom. He's a miserable so and so. Mum says not to trust him. She won't say why.'

'Then there's Demetrius. He hasn't been with us long. He's shifty,' said Natalie.

'Is there anyone at the show, who has a grudge against the gaffer?' asked Pete. The circus children looked at one another. There was something, something left unsaid. The school pals could tell. 'What is it?' asked Pete. 'Have you thought of someone?'

'Well,' said Natalie, 'looking apprehensive. 'It's circus business, I'm not sure that we should say.'

'C'mon,' replied Pete. 'We're friends now, aren't we?'

'Yes, we are,' agreed Natalie, 'but you'll have to promise to keep it quiet – to not repeat it – the adults like to keep their business to themselves.'

'It's Chaos,' said Laurent. 'He drinks. Booze. He's always drunk. He had a falling out with the gaffer last year. The gaffer said he was "unprofessional", said he couldn't be trusted, said he would throw him off the show if he wasn't careful. And what's more, make it his business to make sure he never worked for another circus.'

'Chaos said he had humiliated him, showed him up in front of everyone,' added Yolanda. 'He said he would get even. He hates the gaffer.'

'But why would he get the show into bother?' asked Natalie. 'If the show gets cancelled, he doesn't get paid – just like the rest of us.' It was a good point. It made no sense for Chaos to get the show cancelled, even if he did have a grievance.

'My money's on Demetrius,' said Pete.

'Mine too,' said Timmy. Clive wasn't so sure. He thought this Dave character sounded decidedly dodgy.

'Let's keep an eye on Demetrius then,' suggested Natalie. 'Watch him to see what he might do next.'

It was an exciting idea. The children felt a little like amateur detectives. They decided to dig a little, find out what made Demetrius tick, speak to some others about him. 'Let's ask Tom Parker, to see what he thinks of him,' prompted Timmy. 'We can trust Tom not to tell Demetrius that we have been asking about him.' The children thought this an inspired idea. Tom was a great guy; the circus children looked up to him, and, the school children liked what they had seen so far of the ringmaster.

The decision made, their chat moved to the topic of the disco. 'Will you be coming?'

'Let's give it a whirl,' said Laurent. Pete was pleased. The kiss might be back on. He smiled at Natalie. She smiled back. Did she know what he was thinking? He blushed. Girls, they always seemed to know what was going on in your head. How did they do that?

Friday dawned bright and already hot. The children of Cherry Trees Primary were always excited about the last day of the school year but this one was special, momentous even, for the four school friends were leaving. In September, they would be going to the nearby secondary school. Then, there was the disco to look forward to. Their excitement was near to bubbling over. Children were walking into school with presents for their teachers.

The circus kids felt awkward. They had nothing. They had been here before, of course – at other schools, too numerous to mention – other last days with the gifts that children brought for the staff. Mr Baker smiled at them.

'Don't worry,' he said, 'I didn't expect anything from you kids; you've only been with us a very short time. I've something for you though,' he added, with a grin. In his hand, he held a present of a book for each of them. They looked past him to his desk and spied a whole pile of them. He had one for everyone in the class and they hadn't been overlooked. It made them feel good. *He was okay, this Mr Baker*. It can't have been easy for him, them just rolling up, on the doorstep. No teacher had ever given them anything before. This was different. They liked him for his kindness; no more than that, they *respected* him.

At the end of the day, there were the usual streamers and party poppers. Some of the leavers had brought flour and eggs. It was a tradition. The circus kids had never experienced that before. They were pelted along with everyone else. They laughed. Timmy's face was white with flour. He had been thoroughly dusted; he looked like something out of an episode of *Scooby-Doo*, the school kids' favourite show!

The children made their way home, the circus kids to their caravans, the others to their houses. They had forgotten about Demetrius. There would be time enough for him tomorrow. The circus had reopened and the circus folk were in improved spirits. A large bustling crowd had gathered for the seven o'clock show. They had been attracted by the new posters that had been stuck up in shop windows. As the circus children left the site and headed for the school, they felt happier. A school disco – they had never been to one before; it was time to party!

Seven

First Kiss

The five circus children entered the school hall and were greeted by the sound of deafening pop music. The assembled boys and girls were having to shout to make themselves heard. The hall was dark but there were disco lights flashing out from tall stands from the four corners of the room, like lighthouse beacons at sea. Mr Baker, in open neck flowery shirt, was standing at a double turntable – he was smiling and seemed totally relaxed. It was the end of the school year and the man knew it. The six-week holiday stretched out before them all like the endless rows of deckchairs down on the front.

The teachers were stood together in a huddle, sipping on their drinks. They looked like they had gathered together for safety; like wildebeest on the plains, being tracked by a pride of lions. They were, after all, amid hordes of excitable children, who were intent on having a good time. The hall was decked out in coloured balloons and paper streamers and a large bright banner was strewn across the centre screaming *Good luck to the*

Class of '75! The teachers continued to tap their feet somewhat nervously to the music. "Sugar Baby Love" by The Rubettes was blaring out from the speakers. Bemused, the circus children drank the scene in. They didn't follow the music in the charts. Not having TVs, they never saw *Top Of The Pops*; whereas the school children never missed it (Thursday evenings, seven thirty, BBC1) – they always enjoyed seeing their favourites perform.

Laurent and the other circus children stood to one side, suddenly awkward, uncomfortable – they felt like fish out of water. Then they were spotted by their four school friends, who came over with grins. The boys slapped one another on the back, the girls hugged. Pete saw Natalie for the first time. He smiled at her, she smiled back. He thought she looked drop-dead gorgeous.

'How was the show?' the school kids asked, sounding concerned. 'Had an audience turned up? Did the new posters do their job?' they wondered aloud.

'Yes, it all seems to be okay. Back on track,' said Laurent, trying to sound more confident than he actually was.

'Come and dance,' said Lucy. The girls took to the floor and began to move. The boys stood where they were, rooted to the spot – cue for more backslapping. They were trying to look cool. Why did girls find it so easy to dance? It was embarrassing, this dancing thing. Maybe later, towards the end of the evening, but not yet. It was too early, too light. Pete watched Natalie. He wanted to be talking to her, making her laugh, not stood with the boys, but she was preoccupied with the other girls. She glanced over in his direction. At least, he thought she did.

Mr Baker came over to them. He was beaming. 'Great to see you circus kids here,' he shouted over the music. 'Helping us to celebrate the end of the year, joining in. How are things with the show? I heard there had been some trouble.'

'Yes, some,' shouted back Timmy, 'but it seems to be sorted. We've opened again tonight. There was the usual queue when we left.'

'Look, there's a raffle,' noticed Annie.

'You're lucky with raffles, Lucy,' teased Natalie. Her friend blushed. She still hadn't forgotten the way things had been fixed at the show. The first prize was a watch; it stood prominently on a box in the middle of a display, like a shining jewel in the centre of a tiara. There were soft toys, chocolates and book tokens. Some parents were running the stall, trying doggedly to raise money for the school. The children bought some tickets.

Pete was chatting with Natalie. He was wondering whether he would get an opportunity for a kiss later. Dare he? He had been practising on the back of his hand. He wasn't sure if you were meant to open your mouth, or keep it closed. He had never kissed a girl before – only aunties at Christmas, and then he definitely kept it closed! But with girls, he thought it was meant to be different. It certainly looked different at the cinema. He was nervous, but excited at the thought. A girlfriend, his first. *Would he and Natalie get it together? Would it be tonight?*

The girls went back to dancing. The music was great, upbeat and the sense of fun swept them along. The boys stood around: drinking pop, munching on crisps, telling jokes – boys' stuff, mind you, things that girls wouldn't find funny.

Mark Bolan and T-Rex were playing: "New York City", their latest hit. The lyrics made the children laugh as they sang along about a woman coming out of New York City with a frog in her hand. Bolan, he was one crazy dude!

Natalie came over. 'It's so hot in here,' she said to Pete. 'Shall we go outside and cool down?' *Was this his chance?* They stepped outside and went to sit on a playground bench. The froth of the day had dissipated. They didn't speak. They were trying to guess what the other was thinking. Pete felt awkward; he didn't want to mess up. The silence seemed to go on, and on. Suddenly, Natalie took his hand and leaning forward kissed him gently on the mouth. Their eyes closed; he held on. *Heaven!*

Suddenly, the spell was broken as he was jerked back roughly by the shoulder. It was Laurent. 'What do you think you're doing?' he spat.

'Get off me,' Pete protested, unnerved. Natalie stood up.

'Leave him alone,' she urged. Laurent chose to say nothing. But, taking a swing with his hand, punched Pete square on the face. The older boy then turned on his heels and marched back towards the hall, fists still clenched, knuckles white. Pete rubbed his face. It stung, sore to the touch. Natalie put her arm round him.

'Why did he do that?' asked Pete, fighting back some tears – the last thing he wanted was Natalie to see him blub like some little kid.

'He's wanted to be my boyfriend for ages,' said Natalie quietly, looking just a little sheepish. 'He's jealous.'

'Oh no,' groaned Pete. 'I didn't know.'

'Don't let it bother you, he'll get over it,' she said nonchalantly. Pete wasn't so sure. *Had he ruined things? The kids had all been getting on so well.* 'We'd better get back inside,' said Natalie, pulling him impatiently by the hand.

Pete slowly stood up. *Where was Laurent now? Would he have calmed down? Was he likely to want another go?* With blood trickling down his chin, he felt he stood out like a carrot with a sprouting top.

They walked in apart, not speaking. Clive and Lucy came straight up to Pete, asking him if he was okay. 'I'm fine,' he mumbled.

'But your face,' insisted Lucy, 'your lip is cut.'

'It's nothing,' Pete shrugged. 'Forget it. I have,' he lied.

At that moment, the music stopped and the lights went up. Mr Baker stood resolute at the microphone. His smile had been replaced with a flustered expression. 'Listen, everyone,' he announced tensely. 'I have something disappointing to say. The watch that was the first prize in the raffle, well it's gone missing. It was there one minute, gone the next.'

The children fell silent. *The watch had been stolen. Who would have done such a thing?*

The assembled children in the hall looked round. Their gaze fell on the circus children. They were travellers, not to be trusted their parents said, different to them. It must have been one of them. Yes, that's who it would have been. The circus children seemed to know what they were all thinking. They shifted from one foot to the other, red faced, embarrassed.

Pete stepped forward. He could sense what was being thought. The tension was hot to the touch. 'Listen,' he declared. 'It wouldn't have been one of the circus kids. They're not like that. They can be trusted. They are my friends,' he added with a touch of defiance.

Laurent moved forward and stood by Pete's side. 'We didn't take it. Believe me,' he pleaded. 'Honest.'

Mr Baker stepped forward. 'We don't know who took it,' he announced. 'And, we can't just accuse people.' He looked disappointed. Disappointed about the watch; disappointed too that his Upper Juniors had been so quick to jump to conclusions. 'Whoever has taken it, please return it,' he implored. 'We don't want the evening spoilt now, do we? Let's get back to dancing.' He put on a record.

Laurent turned to Pete. 'Thanks for speaking up for us,' he said, having to shout once more. 'And, sorry about the punch. I was jealous. If Natalie has chosen you, then that's fine with me. I'll get over it!'

'No problem,' said Pete. 'Forget it. We're mates, yes?'

'Yes,' agreed Laurent, 'mates.'

The music went on. It was getting hotter in the hall and the children were tiring, just a little. Suddenly, there was a commotion in the direction of the toilets. Mrs Sampson was walking along, accompanied by a tearstained Kelly Rodgers from 4T, whose face looked red and blotchy.

Mr Baker took to the microphone again. The watch was back. The person who had taken it had shown it to someone else, who had in turn reported it to Mrs Sampson. Kelly Rodgers! Who would have thought it? 'She's always been shifty,' commented Pete. The children took to the dance floor, the boys included. Everyone was up. Mr Baker showed off his moves. The children laughed, so did he.

The raffle was drawn. Lucy didn't win, much to her relief. None of the friends did but they were in such good spirits that they didn't care.

Then suddenly, the disco was over. The evening had sped by. The children of the Upper Juniors said their goodbyes, whereupon the gang of nine friends headed back to the circus camp. There would be time to sit around and chat before the school kids had to be home. Natalie and Pete walked next to each other; they were an item now.

When they got back to the camp, the circus folk were sitting around outside their caravans, relaxing after the show. They were in good spirits, drinking beer and snacking on beef sandwiches – the gaffer's treat. There had been a good-sized crowd and the show had gone well – no hiccups. There was the sound of laughter, lazy, summery giggles. The children sprawled on the grass in front of Olaf and Timmy's caravan. Life was better. Sasha and Gustav were with the cats; they were always with their cats. The children handed round some cans of pop. School holidays – *How absolutely brilliant*! thought the school kids.

'We were going to ask Tom about Demetrius,' Annie reminded them.

'Yes, we were,' said Lucy. 'There's Tom, sitting outside his caravan. Look, he's on his own. Let's speak to him now.' The children ran over.

'Tom,' said Laurent. 'What do you know about Demetrius?'

'Why do you ask?' queried Tom, with a wry smile.

'No reason,' answered Timmy, trying to sound casual but clearly not succeeding.

'Don't give me that,' retorted Tom. 'You don't just suddenly start asking questions about someone. What's he done, poor Demetrius?' The children fell quiet. They didn't like to voice their suspicions – not to an adult. They were thinking back to what Mr Baker had said at the disco, "You can't just accuse people". They suddenly felt mean, then as swiftly, just a little foolish. 'There's nothing wrong with Demetrius,' insisted Tom. 'Well, nothing that a good bath wouldn't sort.' Now Tom was being mean. But he clearly liked his joke, he could not stop laughing. 'Is he your suspect, then? This idiot who tried to tell people the show's visit was cancelled?'

The children flushed red. The ringmaster could see immediately that was exactly what they had been thinking. 'It won't be someone in the show,' he proclaimed confidently. 'It will be an outsider; outside folk are different to us. No offence, kids,' he added, suddenly conscious of the school children's embarrassed faces. Suddenly it was their turn to feel awkward – just like the circus kids had, when the watch had been taken. Surely Tom didn't mean it had been one of them. He seemed to know what they were thinking. 'No, I don't mean it was any of you. You're just kids – the person who spoke to the shopkeepers was a grown man, not a kid.'

'Besides,' said Laurent, 'they like us, they're on our side.' Pete smiled. The trouble between him and Laurent earlier had obviously been forgotten. He was pleased, relieved even. Laurent was bigger than him and he packed a punch. Pete's sore lip was proof of that. Besides, he liked Laurent, whom he thought cool.

The children made their way back to the caravan.

'Well,' said Annie, 'do we still think it could be Demetrius?'

'I like Tom,' said Laurent, 'but I think he's got it wrong this time. The person who tried to get the show's visit cancelled knew where we were going next. Only a circus person would have known that. Tomorrow we meet here early and watch what Demetrius gets up to. If it's him, who knows what he might have planned next? Just because the show went well tonight, doesn't mean this is over.'

The children were agreed. Demetrius could be their man. As they lay in their beds that night, they were still hearing the disco music pounding in their ears, loud, thumping. It had been fun. Maybe things would settle down now. Maybe there would be no more trouble for the show. Little did they know that the next day would bring more twists and turns. Was Demetrius to blame? Or was there someone else hard at work to ruin Templeton's Circus...

Eight

A Disrupted Performance

The next day found the school kids at the campsite early, bright as buttons. It was already hot. They wanted to see what Demetrius might be up to: they were on his case. First though, there were chores to be done, but not just any chores. It wasn't every day you got to help feed a pride of lions. 'How much do they actually eat?' asked Clive, wide-eyed, watching Sasha spear a leg of meat with a pitchfork and shove it under the flap at the bottom of the cage bars. A lioness pounced on it and dragged it into her corner, where she tore into it with powerful jaws.

'We feed them every day except Sunday and Wednesday,' replied Olaf. 'If they were in the wild, they'd always have at least one day without food.' The lions were noisy – the children listened intently to the sounds they were making – more of a moan than a roar – deep moans, each waiting in turn to be fed. Sasha beamed with pride for she was happy to show off her "babies" to the school children.

Cats fed, the children sat down outside Laurent's caravan. From there, they could see the bunk wagon that was home to eight men, including Demetrius. *The men had less space to live than the lions,* thought Clive. Demetrius' bunk was the last one to the left. Its door was shut but the window was open and they could distinguish the shadow of someone moving about inside. 'What shall we do, when he comes out?' queried Lucy.

'Follow him, of course,' the others chorused.

'But we can't all do that, he'll spot us,' countered Lucy. They all wanted to be involved, no-one wanted to be excluded, but they realised that some would have to dip out. They decided to draw lots, it was the fairest way. Lucy and Laurent drew the two longest twigs. They all lolled around on the grass. When would Demetrius show himself? The suspense was killing them.

They didn't have much longer to wait because the window was suddenly pulled shut with a bang and the door opened abruptly. Lucy and Laurent were ready. They jumped up. Giving Demetrius time to be on his way, they inched forward slowly and took up the trail. 'Good luck,' mouthed the others, their eyes glued to the two departing children's route.

Demetrius was a fast walker. The two children had their work cut out just to keep up with him. On the one hand, they didn't want to get too close in case he spied them. On the other, they couldn't just let him slip out of sight. They followed him round the outside of the big top, hopping nimbly over the tent ropes like rabbits as they went. Demetrius went out of the field gate and crossed the road. A bus was coming and he ran to catch it. Laurent and Lucy dashed forward; they jumped on to the bus, just in time to see Demetrius' feet as they disappeared upstairs. The two children went on the bottom deck and took a seat near the back. *Where was Demetrius off to?*

Meanwhile, back at the circus, the remaining children had decided to go and see the ladies in their tent. Manu was there. He looked completely different out of his costume, quite ordinary. He was barking orders at Bruce, clearly unhappy with his groom. The ladies were bobbing their heads vigorously: they seemed to be enjoying their master taking Bruce to task, seemingly agreeing with every word he said.

Manu saw the children and smiled. 'He's lazy,' he said, talking as if Bruce wasn't there. The groom went red and the children felt awkward. They wondered why Bruce let Manu talk about him like that in front of others. Maybe he was frightened of his boss? Maybe he just wanted a quiet life? Manu turned on his heels and marched out of the tent. Bruce looked at the children; he seemed to be daring them to say something, *anything*, so he could answer them back. They kept quiet. They didn't like the look of Bruce. He looked sullen and moody. The groom went back to shovelling dung, muttering under his breath all the while. The elephants seemed pleased to see the children and held out their trunks. But the kids didn't have any treats that day and so the elephants had to go hungry.

The children went back to lying outside on the grass but Sasha spotted them and enquired when her boys were going to do some studying. 'But it's the school holidays,' observed Clive, quietly.

'There is always time enough to work,' answered Sasha. 'In the circus, we know all about work!' Clive didn't like to disagree. He had seen Sasha with the lions; she didn't seem the sort of woman you argued with. The children wondered about Lucy and Laurent. *How were they getting on? Had they managed to keep on Demetrius' heels?*

Laurent and Lucy had remained at the back of the bus, watching who came down the stairs each time they came to a stop. They were soon in the town and Demetrius was suddenly at the doors of the bus, waiting for it to come to a halt. The two children hurriedly ducked down in their seats, in case the hand should look behind him. But he didn't. By now, some of the other passengers were staring at the two children. *What were they up to exactly?* The bus slowed and Demetrius jumped down to the pavement, whereupon the children quickly got up to follow him. He strode down the street and they followed, at a safe distance, darting into shop entrances when he slowed down ahead of them. He headed into a store and they pursued him…

Back at the campsite, time was getting on. It would soon be time for the two o'clock performance. The school children could not help but be excited. They were to be allowed behind the curtains. To them, this seemed more exciting even than being front-of-house. They would get to see the animals and performers prepare away from the public's gaze; it was a secret world and they were to be welcomed in.

They walked into the tent via the back entrance. It was a small space. They could see the back of the bandstand lorry. Tom Parker was everywhere – busy, in charge, commanding like a captain on the deck of his ship. He gave the children a cheeky grin. 'Stay out of the way of the animals, I don't want you kids to be trodden on by an elephant or mown down by the giraffe,' he joked, laughing out loud, but quite serious the children believed, nevertheless.

They spied Chaos. He was in a corner, sitting in front of a mirror, putting his make-up on. It was fascinating to watch. He took such painstaking care. Then he began to brush his luxurious hair. Laurent laughed. 'He takes better care of his locks than the girls on the show; he is always fiddling with his hair, brushing it, shaping it – it's a standing joke amongst the hands.'

'Mama says that he has women's hair,' chipped in Olaf.

'But won't he get covered in foam and stuff?' asked Lucy, 'during the show.'

'No,' replied Timmy. 'The other clowns get covered with slosh, but Chaos stays clean and smart. Mama says she has never known a man so vain.'

Lucy looked at the clown. He seemed an odd character. He drank, was angry with the boss, the gaffer, but still he found time to make sure he looked the business. Chaos caught her staring at him. He scowled and she hurriedly looked away.

There was mounting noise from the big top where the audience was gathering. 'Each performer has to be here, behind the curtain, ready, two acts before their own,' Laurent informed them. 'If they're late, they will be fined. It's Tom Parker's job to announce each act, make sure they have all they need for their performance, and that they are in and out on time.' It seemed an important job. He was akin to a policeman directing traffic.

'He's been a ringmaster for many years,' said Timmy. 'Templeton's is lucky to have him.'

'He's famous in the circus world. He won't stand for any nonsense,' added Natalie. 'He makes sure the circus runs smoothly and that the audience is treated well.'

The children smelt the elephants before they could see them. Suddenly, the tent wall was held open and in squeezed the three beasts, each holding the tail of the animal in front. They seemed even bigger, if that were possible, in this small space; the children pressed back against the tent wall, fearing just a little for their safety. Manu was pulling on the first elephant's ear with a pole that had a hook on the end. Pete though it looked sharp. At a command from Manu, the three elephants slowly lowered themselves down onto the ground, where they sat neatly in a line, kneeling. It was a strange sight. 'But aren't the lions first?' asked Lucy.

'No, remember,' whispered Pete, 'if they are last in one show, they will be first in the next.'

'That's right,' said Natalie. 'Today they're last this afternoon, first this evening. The elephants are on in the first half instead but the flyers will be first.'

At that moment, the four trapeze artists swept into the tent. They had old clothes draped over their sparkly costumes and were wearing dirty clogs. They slipped the footwear off and stripped down to their finery. They began to throw each other in the air by stepping onto one another's cupped hands and then tossing each other over backwards. It made the children gasp. This was just the warm-up, but it made the school children feel quite dizzy.

Tom Parker strode out with a microphone in his hand. 'Is everyone ready?' he barked. 'Yes, then we begin.' He strode through the curtains. The band struck up a bright tune. The crowd clapped and then went quiet, waiting for the ringmaster to speak. The children, on the other side of the curtains, waited. But, nothing came. No word from Tom. There was just a pregnant pause. The children, unable to see, couldn't tell what was happening. The band hurriedly began to play again.

The circus kids looked puzzled. This wasn't what they were expecting. Tom's job was to welcome the audience and then introduce the flyers. Tom strode back through the curtains, red faced. He wasn't at all happy. His eyes practically goggled. 'The microphone,' he complained, 'it's not working. Somebody, check the connection, quick sharp!' A ring boy ran to the amplifier where the microphone was plugged in. He held a dangling wire up in the air. It had been cut; its end was frayed. 'Crikey,' exclaimed Tom, 'it's been tampered with. Hurry, there's a spare out the back.'

The crowd outside had begun to slow handclap. 'Why are we waiting?' some began to sing. Others, at first more polite, then reluctantly joined in, frustrated too. The ring boy ran back in with another lead, but that too had been cut. The children were shocked. *Sabotage!* 'The gaffer has another one in his caravan,' hissed Tom. 'Go fetch it!' The ring boy tore from the tent. The band were still playing, the crowd now booing. They wanted the show to start but it couldn't, not without Tom, its master of ceremonies. The ringmaster looked ready to explode. The elephants stirred; they were used to routine and this wasn't part of the plan. The ring boy pushed his way through the tent flap; he was holding a third microphone. This one had its lead intact. All fingers and thumbs, he hurriedly plugged it into the amplifier and Tom walked through the curtains to immediately take control of the situation. The crowd quietened. He introduced Templeton's Circus with professional aplomb and the flyers strode into the ring. Disaster averted. The children breathed a sigh of relief. The elephants were up on their feet for they were next. Act then followed act, smooth and slick, just as things were meant to be.

The children were mesmerised when George the giraffe entered the tent. He had to lower his long neck to negotiate the back entrance. And then, stretching his front legs wide, he lowered his neck to the ground. Elsie, his rider, pulled up her skirt, and expertly hitched herself backwards onto his neck and, as he raised it, she slid down towards his back, like she was in a playground. It was quite a feat. They felt like applauding, so impressed were they.

The interval came.

Tom came over to the children and asked them how they were finding it. 'It's brilliant,' said Pete, 'even better than watching out front.' Tom laughed and strode out of the tent. The children collapsed to the grassy floor. They were hot but enjoying themselves immensely.

Then suddenly the entire tent was plunged into pitch darkness. Every single light had gone out. The sun outside, as bright as it was, could not penetrate the thick dark tent. There was a shriek from the assembled crowd and a few of the youngest children began to cry. From nowhere, Tom's voice came on through the microphone; it sounded eerie in the darkness, spooky even. 'Stay where you are, stay quite still,' he urged. 'We will try to get the lights back on as soon as possible, but if you start moving you may well trip and fall. Someone will get hurt. Stay calm, stay seated.' There was a hush. There was the odd cry from an infant, but largely there was the silence the commanding Tom had requested. Then the ringmaster's voice came over again on the microphone. 'We can't restore the lights,' he was saying, 'so the ring boys and girls will show the way to walk by shining torches. Don't run! Walk slowly and carefully. If everyone stays calm we will have you out of the tent in no time. The show is over. There will be no second-half. We apologise for any inconvenience.'

There were moans and groans and some shouts of, 'It's a swiz.' Torches began to shine in each corner of the tent and the crowd started to make their way outside into the light. The children too made their exit. Being outback, they didn't have so far to go – they were grateful for small mercies.

Outside, some disgruntled punters had gathered around the box office and were squawking like magpies, demanding their money back. It looked like a veritable storm was brewing. The gaffer and Tom were there trying to calm people down. Try as they might, it looked increasingly ugly. Reluctantly, the gaffer motioned to the box office girls to start handing out refunds. He didn't look happy.

A ring boy came running up. 'The lighting cables had been deliberately disconnected, tampered with,' he informed them. Someone that afternoon had wanted the microphone cut off and the lights put out.

The children flopped down opposite the show front. The crowds were beginning to disperse. A bus pulled up outside of the show and Demetrius hopped off, followed a few seconds later by Laurent and Lucy. He disappeared off through the camp and the two children came and collapsed next to the others. 'Well, that was a complete waste of time,' groaned Lucy. 'All he did was shop. Shop! I ask you.' The children looked at each other and quickly told their two returning friends about the afternoon's events. Someone had been determined to ruin the afternoon's performance and the children realised that it most certainly could not have been Demetrius. But then who?

Nine

Vanity Exposed

Sunday was a day of rest for the circus folk; they always looked forward to it. The Saturday evening performance had gone smoothly but they had been left with a bitter taste in their mouth after the events of the afternoon. The gaffer called a staff meeting at the end of the morning, when practice was over for each of the performers. There was a general sense of dismay and confusion. First, the posters, then the microphone, then complete blackout: who was playing tricks on them and why?

The children met up at midday and talked the situation through. Their prime suspect, Demetrius, had been ruled out of contention. It was time to think again. 'My money is on Chaos,' said Pete. 'He has a grudge. He's bitter and twisted.' It was true, Chaos and the gaffer "had history", as Laurent had put it. But the fact remained that Chaos didn't get paid when the show hit hard times and the circus folk had just seen Saturday afternoon's takings handed back to angry punters.

'Let's watch him today and see what he gets up to,' suggested Yolanda.

'We'll have to be careful,' cautioned Laurent. 'He has a terrible temper and won't take kindly to being spied upon.'

The children were agreed. They would split up to take it in turns to watch Chaos, rather than hanging round in a large group and drawing attention to themselves. Chaos was in his caravan. Pete and Yolanda would sunbathe outside, flicking through a copy of *Look-In* – there was an interview with Lee Majors, the Six Million Dollar Man. Keeping watch, they would see what he did when he came out. But Chaos didn't come out and Pete and Yolanda had nothing to report when the others joined them at tea time.

They decided to play rounders. The circus kids didn't know the game but they had fun learning. It was a good excuse to be all together, but not appear suspicious should Chaos see them. Pete made some tremendous strikes but Laurent, playing a little like Rodney Marsh, threw himself all over and caught people out like nobody's business. A little after six, the clown opened his caravan door and looked out. He saw the children and scowled.

'Charming,' remarked Pete. The boy couldn't get over how someone who made his business making people laugh could be so miserable in real life. Chaos almost fell down the stairs and headed for the big top.

'He's been drinking,' observed Natalie. 'He can hardly walk in a straight line.' Laurent and Pete signalled to the others that they would follow and the two boys set off.

They shadowed the clown to the tent and entering, clambered over the seats to perch in the back row. Chaos had made his way to the centre of the ring where a table had been set. Sitting around it were some of the hands and Gustav, Manu and Tom. They were playing cards and drinking beer.

'What are you two kids up to?' shouted Tom, seeing them.

'Nothing,' replied Laurent. 'Just waiting for the others.'

'Well go wait somewhere else,' answered Manu. 'We're playing cards… for money, and don't want to be disturbed by kids with nothing else better to do.' The men laughed, nodding their agreement with what Manu had said. Kids, there was always something. The two boys got up and sauntered out of the tent, hands in their pockets, whistling. They tried to look casual, not bothered. They couldn't very well stay and besides Chaos was going nowhere, by the looks of it. They found the others and told them what had happened.

'Well there's always tomorrow,' said Yolanda. The children felt deflated, like a balloon from which the air had escaped! 'It's another rest day,' she added. 'We can meet up here and see what he gets up to.'

'Agreed,' chimed Pete, and the others grinned.

The school children walked back home through the warm evening streets. They had only known the circus children a few weeks, but it seemed like they had been friends for much longer. Saying their goodbyes, they went in different directions.

The next morning, the children met up again, all except Yolanda and Natalie whose parents had taken them to the beach. The two sisters hadn't wanted to go for they didn't want to miss out on any excitement, but they could hardly tell their parents what they were up to – grown-ups would have first laughed and then firmly put a stop to their sleuthing. The children again split up, with Timmy and Clive taking first watch, whilst the others went to see what was happening in the zoo.

The two boys sat down on Timmy's caravan steps and waited, chatting and playing a game of cards. Chaos opened his caravan door and hopped down the steps. He was on the move. This was more like it. The boys jumped up and began to follow, some way behind. Chaos walked round the tent and headed out onto the road. He was a fast walker; the boys had to hurry to keep up. The clown walked down the street and crossed the road. They went on a fair way. Chaos went into a distant building with a large front door. The boys caught up. It was a pub. 'That figures,' said Timmy, 'always drinking.'

'Well, we can't go in, children aren't allowed.'

The boys were disappointed. It was hot and they felt like a drink themselves – pop not beer, of course. 'Let's skirt round the back and see if we can see him,' suggested Clive. The boys walked round the pub, through the car park. There was an untidy beer garden out back and they could just about see through the overgrown hedge. They could spy Chaos, who was sitting at a bench, talking hard to a big burly man. 'His friend looks like a nasty piece of work,' said Clive. This was interesting.

The stranger had dark eyes and his face looked chiselled. Chaos slid an envelope towards the man, who pocketed it. Quickly, the hairs on the boys' necks stood up. *What was that all about?* Emptying his glass, the clown stood up. The two men shook hands. Chaos headed back into the pub. 'Look out,' said Clive. 'We'll lose him if we're not careful.' They slid round to the front, and just caught sight of Chaos turning the corner on the other side of the road. The boys hurried after him. It was a fine balancing act: on the one hand, they did not want to be seen, but on the other, could not afford to get left behind. They turned the corner; there he was, on the other side of the road. Suddenly, he stopped and turned round. The boys dived into a shop doorway. *Had he seen them?* No, they thought not, for he had set off again. Clive and Timmy were enjoying themselves. Their adrenaline was pumping. Again, Chaos turned and glanced over his shoulder. *This was a man who was intent on checking he wasn't being followed*, they thought. He was up to no good, the boys were sure of it.

Suddenly, the clown turned into a shop. The boys stopped. What should they do now? How they wished they could tell the others that Chaos was up to something: first meeting the man with menacing features and now the furtive glances, clearly anxious not to be followed. The boys were both wondering the same thing. *What had been in the envelope in the beer garden?*

After what seemed like an age, Chaos emerged with a bag. Had he purchased something? Or maybe collected something? He crossed over but before the boys had time to consider their next move, he jumped into a taxi and was gone. They stood rooted to the spot. Their shoulders sagged as if their arms were weighed down by heavy bags of shopping. What could they do now? It was a bit like the movies, when the hero would jump into the next cab and say "Follow that car". But they had no money and, in any case, they weren't sure people said things like that in real life – and certainly not boys of ten and eleven.

'Let's see what he might have bought,' suggested Clive. 'It could give us a clue to what he intends to do next.' The boys were now convinced that this was their man. They turned into the shop. However, nothing could have prepared them for what they saw. They were standing in the middle of a shop that sold wigs. Yes, wigs. Everywhere they looked, there were hair pieces on wooden busts – in all colours, shapes and sizes. They were confused at first. For one thing, they didn't know such shops existed and secondly, why would Chaos be in one? He had a full head of hair, of which he was proud; he was always fiddling with it, unless… 'The man who just came in,' inquired Clive of the shop assistant, who was now looking at the two boys with an amused face – it wasn't often that children came into his shop.

'Yes,' he answered, 'what about him?'

'Did he, err… buy a wig?' voiced Timmy.

'Yes, that's what people generally do in a wig shop,' the assistant said. The boys could detect the cutting sarcasm in his voice.

'But, he doesn't wear a wig,' said Clive.

'I can assure you,' said the shop assistant, 'that the customer who just left this shop is as bald as a coot and most definitely does wear a wig.' The boys' mouths fell open. That was why Chaos had not wanted to be followed. He was vain, everyone said so. He wouldn't have wanted anyone to know his secret.

The boys walked back to the camp in silence. Their bubble had been burst.

They found the other children. It was late afternoon. The day was still warm, the air parched. Natalie and Yolanda were back from the beach. The children had seen Chaos return and were puzzled not to see the boys too. Clive and Timmy told them their news. Laurent burst out laughing. 'A wig, he wears a wig?' Disappointed, Clive and Timmy couldn't see the funny side. The other children were in fits of giggles.

'You'd never know,' chortled Yolanda. 'He wears very good wigs.' At this, the children roared.

'Listen,' said Natalie, getting a grip of herself. 'There's still the question of the man in the pub and the envelope that Chaos slipped him. Why were they shaking hands? If you ask me, it suggests that Chaos really is up to something.' The others stopped laughing. It was true. This was odd behaviour. What had been in the envelope?

'Money,' offered Laurent. 'Maybe it was money, for a job well done. Paying the stranger for carrying out the sabotage at the show.' The others thought hard. They liked the sound of this. It was an explanation, of sorts. Maybe Chaos was their man, after all.

'Hmm,' said Natalie. 'I wonder if that means the trouble is over. The man has been paid off; it's now finished business. Chaos has got back at the gaffer, debt settled.'

The children sat and pondered. Was this the end? They felt just a little disappointed. They knew they shouldn't. But, they had rather been enjoying the adventure. It had been fun, investigating.

Little did they know, but the trouble for Templeton's Circus had only just begun.

Ten

Unwelcome Headlines

There was an urgent knock at Timmy and Olaf's caravan door. It was early and the boys had only just washed. It was Pete, who didn't look like he had — he looked worried. 'Have you seen the newspaper?' he said, almost shouting.

Timmy shook his head. 'Circus folk don't read newspapers,' he replied. 'They tell stories about your world, not ours.'

'Well, they're telling a story about yours this morning,' insisted Pete and spread the local newspaper out on the caravan table. The children and their parents gathered round. What could be written in the papers about them? They stared down at the newsprint. It screamed out its headline: *Misery Under The Big Top*. They read on:

The Gazette has this week learned of the cruelty that lurks behind the big top of Templeton's Circus, which is pitched in Torquay for a six-week summer run. The circus has been beset with difficulties in the last fortnight:

firstly, it was hit by a false rumour that the show's stay had been cancelled; and then, last Saturday, the afternoon performance had to be halted at the interval due to a power failure. Now, shocking evidence has come to light of the mistreatment of the show's animal stars. A source close to the show has revealed that the circus' three elephants are regularly hit when they fail to perform properly. The source revealed, "It is not unusual for the elephants to be jabbed and poked with a metal bar (known as a bullhook). If they mess up, they are shown the error of their ways! I have heard the elephants squeal in pain when the trainer loses his temper with them. The animals," said the source, "are chained up for long periods of the day with water and food kept in short supply. Elsewhere in the show, lions are reported to be kept in filthy, damp conditions, with mistreatment again alleged. If a lion doesn't want to do something it will be punished – either through feeling the lash of a whip or a poke with a bar," claimed the source. The circus' two bears are also said to be regularly beaten. Dave Quinn, spokesman of Torquay's Friends Against the Circus (TFAC) said, "Templeton's Circus is no friend to animals. It seeks to make money from creatures that it can only control through the use of violence and aggression. We urge the good people of Torquay to vote with their feet and boycott the show."

Sasha began to cry. As she re-read the article, the words seemed to jump about on the page. She was shaking, uncontrollably. Gustav put his arm around her. 'But, I don't understand,' she sobbed. 'Who would have said such things? What do they mean by a source? Do they mean someone here at the show? One of us? Everyone knows that we care for our lions like they were our children. Dirty conditions? Why, their cages are spotless. We do not whip or beat our babies with bars. They do a trick well, they get a titbit. Simple – we treat our animals with kindness. All the roaring they do, the whips, that is just for show, what the public want – danger. It is not meant, there is no harm in it.'

'And what about Manu's elephants?' said Timmy. 'He would no sooner harm them than we would our lions.'

'And then there are the bears,' said Pete. 'Don't forget them.' None of the circus folk spoke, which he found odd.

Pete went quiet. He didn't like the life that he saw the circus animals leading: the hours the cats spent cooped up in their cages; or the time the elephants spent chained to the boards in their tent. But he had never seen the circus folk mistreat one of their animals. They were forceful with them at times, it was true: you couldn't just nicely ask an elephant or lion to do something, you had to show them who was boss. His dad did that with their dog, Ben. But that didn't mean cruelty. No, he was sure, none of the circus people would be deliberately mean to one of their creatures.

'We must show this to the gaffer and Tom,' said Olaf.

'And to Manu,' added Gustav. 'He needs to know what has been said about him; he treats his ladies with love and affection. "Squealing in pain" – what nonsense!'

They went to Manu first. It seemed only fair. He went white, then red. He looked fit to explode, with eyes bulging out of his face; he kicked the side of his caravan, in temper. 'Calm down,' pleaded Sasha, sounding just a little desperate. 'I know how you are feeling but we must think. Don't be the person who is described in the newspaper. You're better than that. Think! Who might have said these things?'

'Bruce,' spat Manu. 'I've never trusted that no good layabout. Wait till I get my hands on him.'

'But why would he do such a thing?' questioned Gustav.

'Who knows what makes him tick,' answered Manu. 'But I don't trust him, never have.'

Sasha nodded. 'You're right not to trust him,' she said. She suddenly looked embarrassed. 'I've never said before, but I caught him taking money from the girls who sell the programmes.'

'You never said,' said Gustav.

Sasha looked ashamed. 'I was frightened,' she said. 'He promised to make trouble for me if I said anything. I couldn't even tell you, my husband.' For the second time that morning, she began to cry. Olaf and Timmy looked on edge; it wasn't nice to see your mum crying. They felt rather helpless.

'To the gaffer!' said Gustav. 'He needs to be told.' They rushed down the steps of Manu's caravan and tore to the gaffer's long, luxurious trailer – all except Manu, who mumbled something about finding Bruce and hotfooted it instead in the direction of the elephant tent.

The gaffer was in. He stood reading the paper with his back turned. He wheeled round to face them. 'Who is this person who wants to destroy my circus?' he asked, in anger, pacing the length of his caravan. 'First it was the posters, then Saturday's show, now these lies.' Pete wanted to voice the children's suspicions about Chaos but thought better of it. The gaffer would go off on one at the mention of the clown's name; there was no love lost there and Pete wanted to talk things over with the others first.

The children left the adults to moan and groan and slipped away to find the rest of the gang, Natalie, Yolanda and Laurent. They assembled at Timmy and Olaf's caravan steps. Could it have been Chaos? Was he meeting a reporter that day in the beer garden? Had what he passed him in the envelope been the lies that the town of Torquay were waking up to that morning in their newspaper? Or was Chaos the innocent party and Bruce the guilty one?

'What should we do?' asked Yolanda.

'I think we should tell Tom our suspicions about Chaos – about the meeting between him and that nasty looking stranger,' said her sister, firmly. *What was in that envelope?* The children thought hard about the possibilities.

'I'm not so sure about telling Tom,' mused Laurent. 'Look how he reacted when we mentioned Demetrius to him. We can't go round accusing first one person, then the next. We have to be sure of our facts.' The children were joined by Lucy, Clive and Annie. The circus kids and Pete filled them in on what had happened.

Clive came up with an interesting idea. 'The gaffer should invite the newspaper to send a reporter down to see the animals, their cages – the kindness that the trainers use.' The children thought this a great notion.

'Why didn't I think of that?' said Laurent. 'To fight back, putting the record straight – it's just what the doctor ordered.'

'Let's suggest it to Tom,' urged Yolanda. 'C'mon.' The children ran to Tom's caravan, but he wasn't there. They were disappointed.

'He'll be with the gaffer,' said Laurent. Sure enough, the children found Tom, Sasha, Gustav and Manu, deep in conversation outside the Gaffer's caravan. 'Listen,' pleaded Laurent. 'We have an idea.' They hurriedly put it to them. The grown-ups listened.

'It's a fantastic idea,' nodded Tom in enthusiastic agreement. 'You kids have really got something there.'

The gaffer agreed enthusiastically. 'I'll go to the newspaper's offices this minute. We'll get a reporter down this afternoon.' He disappeared back into his caravan, then quickly reappeared, practically running down the steps and set off in the direction of the town. Sasha and Gustav headed for the lions' van. There were no prizes for guessing what they were going to do. They would scrub the van from top to bottom; not that they needed to – it was always clean.

'Did you find Bruce?' Pete asked Manu.

'No sign of the good-for-nothin',' spat Manu. The children looked at one another. Was Bruce the one? He would certainly have known where the show was headed next; the man who had ruined the posters knew that. He could have tampered with the microphones and cut the power to the lights at Saturday's afternoon performance. No, people wouldn't have been suspicious to see him moving around behind the scenes of the show. Elsewhere, he could have been the newspaper's source – the person who had told such hateful lies.

The children sat down on the grass and thought about the events of the morning. Things seemed to be moving so fast. It was like being on a runaway train. It was hard to think what might happen next.

A while later, the gaffer returned. He was accompanied by a young man who was holding a pad and pen, a camera draped round his neck like a weapon – he looked like a reporter if ever there was one. Tom stepped forward, oozing charm like treacle. He really was so good at dealing with people. The reporter was to get the full works – a tour of the show, behind the scenes. 'We have nothing to hide,' they heard Tom declare boldly. 'We are proud of our animals and show folk.' The children tagged along. It was fun to watch Tom at work. He had the patter of a used car salesman. He knew just what to say, and what to show the reporter. He showed off Manu who stroked the elephants and tickled them behind the ears. He showed Sasha rubbing her cats' cheeks, the great beasts purring in delight. The reporter took photos and spoke to people who worked on the show. He also spoke to punters who were making their way round the zoo. He seemed to be doing a lot of smiling and things looked like they were going well. At the end of the tour he shook hands with the gaffer and Tom, who both looked like relieved men.

That night the gaffer sent sandwiches to all the circus folk. He wanted to give them a lift. He cared about them and didn't like to see them under attack. The school children were invited to share in the feast. People were full of praise for Clive, who had come up with the idea of getting the reporter down to the site. The school kids were proud of their friend. Tom was doing the rounds, talking with people, laughing, smiling.

Bruce had returned to the ground in the late afternoon. He had been at the pub. He seemed genuinely surprised when Manu confronted him. No, he hadn't said anything to the newspapers, he insisted. The gaffer and Tom said they believed him. Manu wasn't so sure. 'Just so you know,' the elephant trainer said to him, 'I'll be watching you very closely from now on.'

The folk at Templeton's Circus found it difficult to get off to sleep that night. Their brains were buzzing. What would the newspapers say, the following day? Would it be enough to keep the public from turning against the show? For the children, Chaos and Bruce remained in the frame: was one of these two the enemy within?

Eleven

Haircut

The school kids were at the campsite early on Tuesday morning. They had bought a copy of the morning newspaper with them but were disappointed to find that there was no mention of the circus in its pages. 'Maybe it will be in the later edition,' suggested Clive. 'There's always a second edition each day at about twelve o'clock.' Hmm, it seemed a long time to wait. What to do?

It being the holidays, there were two shows every weekday, bar Monday, at two thirty and seven thirty. The children wondered if the crowd would be down today. *Would people stay away because of what they had read the day before?* The circus folk were tense, they could tell. They were making their way about their business, stern faced. Manu could be heard shouting at Bruce. Tom walked past. 'What are you up to?' he asked with a smile. Tom always had a smile, no matter what.

'We thought there would be something in the newspaper,' said Laurent. 'But, there's nothing.'

'The reporter was too late for the morning run,' replied Tom. 'There'll be something in the later one. We need it. Can't have our show ruined, can we?' He looked at the children. They needed a distraction, he could tell. 'Why not go get that haircut, you've been talking about Olaf?' Tom said, with a mischievous grin. The children looked at Olaf. He had been talking about a Mohican for the past two weeks, ever since arriving in Torquay. *Dare he? What would his father, Gustav, say?*

'How much would it cost?' enquired Olaf.

Tom handed him a pound note. 'Go treat yourself,' he said. 'We could do with something to make us smile.' Olaf felt the crisp note in his hand. Tom really was a good friend to the circus children. They were incredibly fond of him; but more than that, they respected him – he was always so strong and calm, even in the midst of all the trouble they had experienced recently. He had been the one to keep them all positive, not panicking. Level-headed.

The children looked at Olaf. 'Come on,' he said jumping up. 'What are we waiting for?' They headed for a barber's that the school kids knew in town. It was but a short walk away. They walked in.

The barber looked up from the magazine that he was sat reading. 'How can I help, kids?' he asked. 'Who's for the chop?'

'I've come for a Mohican,' said Olaf, sounding very grown up. 'I have a pound.'

'You'll get some change,' said the barber, smiling. 'Take a seat, kids. This will take a little time.' The children fell into the chairs around them. This was fun. They had forgotten that the circus was in trouble; they were enjoying themselves. *What would Olaf look like? What would his parents say?*

The barber took out clippers and began to shave the hair at either side of Olaf's head. He went in smooth strokes. It reminded Pete of a sheep being shorn. The boy's hair fell to the floor in piles. Olaf was left with a strip of hair running down the middle of his head. It looked funny, out of place. Then taking the scissors, the barber cut the hair on the strip, but not too short. Then finally, taking lots of cream, he began to pull the hair up on end until it stood pointing to the ceiling. It looked great. Different. Cool.

The barber handed him a tub of Brylcreme. 'You'll need that to make it stiff enough to stand on end,' he advised, knowledgeably. They walked out into the sunshine. They couldn't stop looking at Olaf. He looked great! Olaf stopped to look in the shop window. He could see his reflection. He looked fifteen, at least. They walked on, laughing.

'Look,' said Clive stopping outside the newsagent. There was an advert for the afternoon paper. The headline was about the show. A poster for the newspaper shouted, *Tempelton's Circus Fights Back.* They bought a copy and sitting on a bench began to pore over the front page article. Laurent, the eldest, read it out loud:

Templeton's: A circus under threat!

A Special Report by Dan Foley, your Ace Investigator

Following on from the stories of animal cruelty that surfaced yesterday, the Gazette was granted unlimited access behind the scenes of Templeton's Circus. Ringmaster, Tom Parker, forty-two, showed me around the stables of the show and I was able to see for myself how these magnificent animals are treated. What did I find? Well, I saw no signs of trainers being rough with animals, as a mystery source close to the show had claimed. But then again, Reader, would I have done? The circus folk would surely be on their best behaviour in front of a reporter from the Gazette. It is true that the lions' cage seemed spotlessly clean, a far cry from the dirty conditions that had been alleged. Mr Parker went to great lengths to reassure me that the animals at Templeton's show, in Torquay for a further four weeks, are part of the family. Manu Adewele, elephant trainer, thirty-seven, said, "I would no sooner hurt my elephants than one of my children." Mr Adewele stroked his elephants throughout my interview with him. The creatures seemed relaxed enough. One thing's for sure, the next few days will be important for the show. It may struggle to make a success of its stay in the town after a series of mishaps that first saw posters tampered with and then a performance cancelled at half time.

Have you been to the show? How did you feel the animals were treated?

Write to the Editor.

The children looked at one another. They were disappointed. The article had not been as friendly to the circus as they had hoped. 'Why does the reporter have to go on again about the problems we have faced?' complained Laurent bitterly.

The children walked back to the show ground, despondent. They went to find Tom, but he wasn't in his caravan. There was the sound of heated voices coming from the tent. The circus folk had gathered and were discussing the newspaper article, which the gaffer had already shared with them. The children walked into the tent. They stopped talking when they saw the children then, despite themselves, many began to laugh. They were looking at Olaf, his hair. The children had forgotten. A few of the grown-ups came to pat him on the back. 'You look great,' one laughed. 'We needed a giggle!'

Gustav emerged from the crowd. He didn't look pleased. 'I told you to always be sensebelle,' he despaired.

Tom motioned for the crowd to settle down. 'Look,' he said. 'We can either sit back and take all this nonsense that is happening to us. Or we fight back. I say we fight.'

There were shouts of 'Yes,' and 'Let's!'

'But what can we do?' asked Sasha.

'I have an idea,' blurted out Lucy. The circus folk turned to look at her. How could this tot of a girl, an outsider, have an idea worth listening to when they, the adults, were stumped?

'Let her speak,' declared Tom. 'These children are our friends.' Lucy turned red. She didn't like the fact that everyone was now staring at her.

'Go on,' said Pete. 'What is it? You have to say now.'

'Why don't you parade the elephants down to the beach, let them bathe in the sea,' she suggested. 'I saw elephants parading through a town once; it might work...' Her voice faltered. There was a silence. It was an unexpected thought. Could it be done?

'I like the idea,' shouted Tom. 'It will give the people of Torquay a chance to see how we love our animals. The beach is always packed with holidaymakers. It would cause a real stir!'

'Let's get a film crew there from the local TV station, get ourselves on the local news,' added the gaffer. 'It will be great publicity.'

'What do you say, Manu?' Tom asked. 'Could we do it?'

'Of course,' said Manu. 'My ladies will love it. And I shall ride on a horse alongside them. We will bring the circus to the people of Torquay!' There was an excited buzz amongst the assembled performers and circus hands. This was different; they hadn't done it before.

Manu and Tom strode off to the elephant tent, deep in discussion. The children looked at one another. 'Will you have to inform the police?' asked Pete.

'Circus folk don't trust the police,' answered Timmy. 'They always side with the cranks.'

'But,' said Pete, 'won't they have to shut off roads and stuff? Can you just take three elephants for a walk?'

'We can do anything,' said Laurent. 'We're circus!' Pete frowned. He wasn't so sure. But he could see the circus children were pumped.

Quickly, the grooms were organised and Bruce appeared leading the three elephants out of the tent. They walked quickly, each holding on to the tail in front of them. Manu, as if by magic, appeared in full costume, sitting astride a Palomino horse. Chaos and the other clowns had rushed to get into their outfits; they were to lead the way. And then, before anyone had a chance for second thoughts, they were off. The lead elephant, Flossie, negotiated her exit from the gate without any hesitancy. The children ran along the pavement, keeping pace with the elephants, which were going at a tremendous speed. Cars had to slow down and before long a queue of traffic was bringing up the rear. Children came out of the houses as a shout went up down the road, 'There are elephants in our street!' A police car drew up but Tom, with his usual charm, seemed to handle the officers easily enough. Then the sea came into view. The elephants were beginning to trumpet for they were excited. The school children laughed to see Bruce scurrying behind with a shovel, sweeping up dung that the beasts were now depositing on the streets of Torquay at regular intervals. Manu jumped off the horse and took hold of Flossie with his bull hook. He turned her in the direction of the sand. The crowd of sunbathers quickly dispersed; no-one wanted to argue with a ton of elephants, and then the three animals plunged into the water. Manu, in all his finery, and Bruce, went wading in after them. The massive beasts slowly lay down on their sides and let the water run over them. The sound of their trumpeting was piercing. They were enjoying themselves, like never before. A crowd of a hundred or more had gathered to watch. Soon it was two or three hundred, as people from the town, getting wind of events – and of the elephants themselves – made their way down to see what all the excitement was about.

A television crew arrived and Tom took centre stage, telling the reporter about the care the circus took with its animals, inviting viewers to judge for themselves just how well they were treated. The sight of elephants squirting water into the air from their trunks, spoke volumes. People smiled to see the animals so obviously enjoying themselves in the sunshine.

After an hour or so, Tom signalled that it was time to head back home. The elephants were reluctant to leave the water, but Manu seemed to have thought of this and produced carrots to tempt them out on to the sand. Then he shouted a command and they linked tails and set off, at a slower pace this time, tired from their exploits.

A crowd followed them back to the ground, fully intending to go to the five o'clock performance.

Lucy's idea had been an unqualified success. That week the circus played to packed houses. People had seen the item on the local news. Tom Parker and the gaffer beamed. The circus folk were happy. Maybe things were turning in their favour? However, the enemy, whoever they might be, was not finished yet, as the circus folk were soon to discover…

Twelve

Horror Under The Big Top

Natalie had been crying. Pete could tell. 'What is it?' he asked.

'Nothing. I mean, I can't say.'

Pete went quiet. Girls! If it wasn't one thing, it was another. They sat there on the caravan step in silence. It was Saturday morning; there were only three weeks of the circus' stay left. Pete didn't like to think about the time when Natalie would be moving on. He would be losing his first girlfriend. It would also mean it was nearly time for the return to school. He tried again. 'You can trust me, honest. If something's upsetting you, I might be able to help.'

The caravan door opened. Yolanda stepped out. She climbed over them, without a word. Odd, he thought. She was usually chatty and bright. Maybe that was something to do with it. Had the sisters fallen out? 'Is it Yolanda?' asked Pete. 'Have you had an argument?'

'It's all of them,' said Natalie, her bottom lip trembling. 'I told them that I thought there was no place for animal acts in a modern circus. It's cruel to keep things chained up or in cages. Mum and Dad went mad; said I didn't know what I was talking about; said I was to keep quiet and not let the others catch me talking like that.'

Pete sighed. The circus was a complicated place. So many people, all trying to get on and live cheek by jowl in one small place; and as for the animals, well he thought they would be better off in a proper zoo, or better still, the wild.

Yolanda came running up. 'Come on, Nat,' she begged. 'Cheer up, Mum and Dad will get over it. It's just a falling out. Don't mention the animals again, and things will calm down.'

The other kids came strolling along. They were in good spirits. Relaxed in the sunshine, nothing had gone wrong at the show for a week. Maybe it had been Chaos, and now he saw the debt as repaid. 'The hatchet's buried,' as Pete's mum would say.

There was movement in the camp. It was coming up to midday. After a spot of lunch, the circus folk would begin preparing for the two o'clock show. The school kids were invited to eat with Sasha and Gustav and the boys had bacon sandwiches, huge doorstep ones.

The cats were to be first that afternoon. Chaos the Clown would do his opening spot, where he would be putting on his makeup in the ring cage, only for a spotlight to find the toy lion on a stool. The children remembered that Chaos would pretend to look scared, then grab the toy and exit before the lions made their entrance. It was a great way to start the performance. The children were stood waiting in the zoo. The first lioness to run down the cage tunnel to the ring was always Tracey. In the darkness of the tent, she would sit by the door to the ring cage waiting patiently for Chaos to do his thing; then when he left, the cage door would be shut, the tunnel gate raised, and she would run in – soon to be followed by each lion – released from the wagon to run down the tunnel into the ring. Sasha was talking to Tracey, who was chuffing. At a signal from Gustav, who stood a way along the tunnel, she raised the wagon cage door and Tracey jumped down onto a stool and then down into the tunnel. She ran into the big top. The children could hear the audience laughing. The spotlight would be on Chaos and he would be pretending to look scared of the toy lion.

Suddenly there was an ear-piercing scream. That wasn't in the script. Something had gone wrong! Sasha ran into the big top, quickly followed by the children. Gustav was entering the cage with a large pole. In one corner, with his back to the audience, stood Chaos, blood dripping from his fingers. Tracey was in the cage with him, roaring and snatching. She grabbed the clown by the arm and pulled him down to the floor. Sasha ran at Tracey with a pole and two ring boys aimed water from fire extinguishers in her direction. The lioness was soaked. She released her grip on Chaos and Gustav chased her out of the cage and back down the tunnel, hind legs in the air, towards the beast wagon.

The lights had gone up. Tom Parker took to the microphone. 'Ladies and gentleman,' he said. 'Do not panic. The lion is back in its cage.'

There was the sound of a loud bang from the zoo. It silenced the crowd – some realised that they had just heard a gunshot. What was happening now? Could someone really be shooting? Clive, Natalie and Laurent ran out through the ring entrance into the zoo. Gustav was standing there, with a smoking gun in his hand. Tracey was lying motionless on the grass of the ring tunnel; the children knew straight away that she was dead. The lions were going crazy, roaring and jumping at the bars of their wagon. Sasha was shutting down the sides of the lorry as quickly as she could. Darkness, she shouted, would calm them down.

Meanwhile in the tent, Chaos had been lifted out of the cage and carried outback. He was bleeding badly from his arm, his shirt soaked in blood. Tom Parker was in charge. 'Put him down gently,' he said. Someone had run to the nearest telephone box, to call for an ambulance. Chaos appeared to be drifting in and out of consciousness. A ring hand had tied a band tightly round the top of his arm to stem the flow of blood.

Lucy felt sick. This was awful. The lions had always seemed controlled, safe even; now things had gone badly wrong. *Was Chaos dying?* the children wondered. *Here, now, right in front of them?* They had never seen anyone hurt like this before. 'He'll be all right,' said Tom in a hushed voice. 'Chaos,' he urged, 'stay with us, my friend.

Stay with us.' He tapped the clown lightly on the face. Chaos stirred. Then he closed his eyes again.

The sound of a siren came on the afternoon air, then another. It was an ambulance, followed quickly by two police cars and a motorbike. The ambulance men bundled out of the van and gathered round the injured clown, who looked like a crumpled piece of clothing, which needed ironing. They tightened the band round his arm and lifted him gently onto a stretcher and placed an oxygen mask over his mouth. They calmly put him into the ambulance and eased away from the site, with the police motorbike riding pillion.

The show had come to an abrupt end and the ring boys were showing the crowd out of the big top; people spilled onto the grassy area outside the tent. Despite their disappointment, they were quiet. They realised that things had gone badly wrong and that a man's life must now be in danger, if he wasn't already dead. The ring boys ushered them through the gates with requests of 'Pass along please. Our performer will be okay, he's just taken a bad injury. He'll live.' Tom had told them what to say. There was confusion. Some people did not want to go; they sensed there would be more happening.

Back in the zoo, Sasha was sobbing. The lioness, Tracy, was being lifted out of the ring tunnel and was placed onto a waiting wooden trolley. The gaffer was overseeing things, Tom still busy with the punters outside.

'Whatever happened?' said Laurent to Gustav, outraged that a cat had been shot.

'In the darkness, someone lifted the tunnel gate and let Tracey into the cage with Chaos still in it. Poor blighter! He could have been killed. And we've lost one of our lions. I had to shoot her because she was going crazy in the ring tunnel – out of control. I simply had to shoot her! I thought she might break out.' The lioness lay limp on the trolley. Her eyes glassy, her mouth open, her paws hanging off the end. It took five ring boys to pull the trolley, such was her size.

The children fell down on the grass like lead weights. After a week of calm, disaster had struck the show once again. And Chaos, who had been their latest suspect, was in an ambulance on his way to hospital. Tom Parker strode round the side of the wagon. 'It was when the lights were down, only a spotlight on Chaos; that's when the villain struck.' The gaffer disappeared into his caravan flanked by three policemen. This was bad. The children realised it. So much of circus life was dangerous but you could forget that danger when the trainers and performers delivered their acts, night after night, without problems.

Two policemen had come out of the caravan. They spoke with Tom. 'They want everyone to assemble in the big top,' he shouted. 'Spread the word. They want to interview everyone. You school kids had better get off – this is no place for you. News of the incident was bound to be reported on the local radio; your parents might hear and would then be worried.'

The children said their goodbyes and wandered back to the front of the show. There were still people gathered round. Some smoking, others laughing nervously. The children looked at them scornfully. *What was there to laugh about?* A man was seriously injured and a beautiful creature was lying dead.

Ring boys were out front, putting the now familiar *Cancelled* signs against the seven thirty show signs. As they made their way through the gate, the children passed the reporter, Dan Grayson. He was heading into the show, his pen and notebook poised. 'More bad publicity,' said Clive. 'Templeton's Circus is in serious trouble.' The children felt sorry for Tom and the rest of the circus folk, but most of all they felt sorry for Chaos and of course Sasha, who had lost one of her "beloved babies" that afternoon.

The police set to. Each performer went into the ring, where two tables with chairs had been placed opposite one another – it was time for interrogation. Statements were taken in turn from each person, with the circus folk making two quiet queues; there didn't seem much to say. It was a nightmare.

Where had they been when the act had gone wrong? What had they seen? Heard? What did they know?

Later, Tom and the gaffer were both interviewed separately. They were asked, *Who might be trying to ruin the show? What suspicions did they have?* Neither man could think of anyone to blame apart from the cranks – they liked trouble. They were against the circus – always against the circus.

Dave, the leading anti was interviewed down at the station. But, he had been outside the big top all afternoon, protesting in full view of a number of people. He was incandescent with rage: he didn't want to talk about Chaos; he was focusing on the fact that a lioness had been "murdered". Were the police going to bring charges against Gustav for shooting the lion? He wanted to know. If not, why not?

Night-time came. The circus folk gathered in the tent. The gaffer addressed them in the glow of the ring lighting. The police would be back tomorrow; there were more questions they wanted to ask. But, he said the show would go on. They would be missing a lion and a clown, but they could not afford to shut up shop. No-one would get paid if they didn't carry on and the circus would go belly-up. They must be on their guard. The performers and ring hands gave him a loud round of applause. Some even punched the air in defiance.

They wandered back to their caravans that evening, utterly drained. The shutters on the lions' wagon were back up and the lions sat behind the bars, sleepily, as if nothing had happened; Tracey's compartment in the cage stood empty. Sasha and Gustav sat up with their boys long into the night: chatting, crying, trying to comfort one another. Later, much later, they clambered into bed.

Nothing could have prepared the circus folk for what was going to happen next. They were to be surprised and for the first time, the "enemy within" might just have made a mistake.

Thirteen

A Visit to the Hospital

When the school children arrived at the camp mid-morning, there was already a police car parked ominously outside the gaffer's caravan. The children found their circus friends, who were sitting outside the ladies' tent. They looked glum. What news was there? Gustav and Sasha had been summoned to the gaffer early that morning. The police had drawn a blank: no-one had seen anyone in the darkness. The police had no leads, nothing to go on.

'Well, one thing's for sure. Chaos isn't our man,' declared Pete. The children nodded. Their most recent suspect was lying in a hospital bed so it certainly hadn't been the clown who had been causing trouble for the show.

'I wonder how he's doing?' said Lucy. The children were feeling guilty that they had suspected poor Chaos. They were remembering that they had followed him, spied on him. They felt awkward.

'We could visit him?' suggested Clive. 'Take him something, show him we care. It's what people do.' The children thought this a good idea.

'We can't all go,' said Natalie. They decided that Laurent, Pete and Natalie would make the journey across town. Tom told them which hospital the clown had been taken to.

'Afternoons are visiting time in hospitals,' Clive informed them. He knew from when his auntie had been ill. The school kids headed for home, with Pete agreeing to meet Natalie and Laurent at the bus station at two o'clock. From there, they would travel to the hospital, which was on the other side of town.

The bus journey was long. The three friends made their way to Ward C, where Chaos had been placed. They walked along, their eyes jumping from bed to bed; then they spotted the clown, who was sitting up in bed. He wasn't wearing his wig. The children stared at his bald head, and then their eyes moved to his arm, which was heavily bandaged. 'Hello kids,' he said. Surprisingly, he seemed really pleased to see them. His eyes were large and bright, like two fried eggs. 'Nice to see some faces that I know,' he laughed. Pete had brought some grapes. It was what grown-ups did. He put them on the bedside table. 'I'd rather it was a bottle of Scotch,' joked the clown. It was odd. Chaos was usually a miserable so and so, but here he was, a day after a brush with death, and he seemed happier than they had ever seen him before. Weird. The children drew up some chairs and sat at his bedside.

'How are you feeling?' asked Laurent.

'Not too bad, considering,' replied Chaos. 'Truth be told, I'm feeling incredibly lucky. I could have been a goner; if it hadn't been for the fire extinguishers, and Gustav with his pole, well she could have done for me. The local paper want to run a feature on me – "The Clown Who Lived", they are going to call it.' He looked pleased with himself.

The children shifted awkwardly on the palms of their hands. They exchanged looks. They had discussed it on the bus and decided to say sorry to the clown, for suspecting him. They felt they should. It was Laurent, who finally spoke up, 'Look,' he said. 'We owe you an apology.' He began to explain how they had suspected Chaos: following him that day to the beer garden; the shifty looking stranger and the envelope; the clown's grudge against the gaffer; even the visit to the wig shop. To their amazement, Chaos began to laugh – out loud – like, really big guffaws. The children were relieved, if not a little puzzled. This was a new Chaos. He was acting out of character. He seemed so relaxed about everything.

'Look,' he said. 'I'll let you into a secret. I have been losing money at cards lately. I borrowed money from a loan shark. I was giving him back what I owed him in the beer garden. The gaffer lent me the money to pay him off, to get him off my back; that geezer was a nasty bit of work. The gaffer has been good to me. Yes, we had a falling out a few years back. He could have kicked me off the show then, but he didn't. I owe him everything. I wouldn't want to see Templeton's go down the tubes. It's my life.'

He suddenly looked tired. As if the effort of talking to the children had worn him out. They remembered that he was a man who had suffered a serious injury only the day before. They should go. Let him rest. The clown had fallen asleep and the children got up quietly and made their way back down the ward.

'How was he?' enquired the nurse at the desk, looking up over her glasses.

'It was odd,' replied Pete. 'He seemed more cheerful than usual, brighter – happy even.'

'He's had a shock – it makes people re-evaluate! Plus, he has been given some pretty strong painkillers; they make you a bit heady.'

The circus children couldn't help but wish that Chaos would stay his new self – it would be better to have him that way. But they wondered if he would go back to being a miserable so and so when the medication had worn off.

'So he doesn't bear a grudge against the gaffer,' observed Natalie. 'We were wrong.'

The children were quiet on the way back home: the enemy was not only still out there, but he had stepped up his game and they were right back to square one – no suspect, other than Bruce, and they still didn't know why he might want to destroy the show. This detective work was tiring stuff. They knew that people didn't do things without a reason. If Bruce was their man, they would have to work out why he would be acting in such a way. Maybe they should voice their suspicions to the police.

But when they came to think about it, what did they have to say? Yes, Bruce seemed unhappy in his work. But that didn't mean anything in particular.

The children arrived back at the camp and were greeted by an unexpected scene. There were punters everywhere; the zoo was teaming with people – like ants around their nest hole. A huge crowd had gathered around the lion lorry; they stood there gawping at the five beautiful beasts. Sasha was there, chatting to some of the people. She half-smiled when she saw the children. 'It's odd, isn't it,' she whispered to them. 'The person setting out to ruin the show wouldn't have seen this coming. News of Tracey's attack on Chaos has brought them all out, like wasps on a hot day. They can't get enough of the circus. Bookings for this week have gone through the roof, most performances are sold out. The gaffer's delighted!' The children looked at one another. *Good news,* they thought, and they needed some.

The circus folk were all smiles. Their show had never been so popular. This meant takings would be up and the gaffer always gave them a cash bonus when the show did well. The day wore on with a steady flow of visitors to see the animals.

In the evening, the children gathered around Natalie and Yolanda's caravan. Their parents, Orlando and Toni, were very musical and soon the children were singing along to an instrumental accompaniment. Other folk came and joined them, squatting down on the threadbare grass. There was the smell of cooking, as the circus folk enjoyed a meal outside. Tom stopped by. He looked drained, as grey as dust. 'It's been a busy day,' he commented. 'I've had police and reporters to speak to. Everybody wants a piece of us at the moment.'

'But, that's good, isn't it?' enquired Pete.

'Could be,' said Tom. 'But, the police are beginning to ask awkward questions about the safety of the punters visiting the show. The chief constable is nervous about someone else getting injured by a "wild beast". If we can't assure them that there is no threat to the public, they may shut us down, or at the very least, move us on.'

The children fell silent. This was bad news at the end of what had been such a lovely day. Tom grimaced. 'The police are coming back in the morning to have a further look around. The gaffer is not pleased. Well, I'm for my bed,' he said. 'Goodnight kids.' It was time too that the school kids were making their way home. They bade their farewells and headed for the road.

In the morning, Sasha and Gustav were very busy. They had just a day to get ready for the Tuesday performance. The lions would need to learn a new way of working. There was no Tracey. Where she had taken her turn to perform tricks before, the other lions now had to do more. Sasha and Gustav were always patient with their cats. They used long sticks as a kind of extension to their arms – pointing to where they wanted the lions to go. Each trick was rewarded with a knob of meat from a pole. The lions were trained with patience and love, but even then they could be difficult. This morning, they were unsettled. Were they missing Tracey? Did they wonder where she had gone? Did lions even think like that? The children weren't sure.

Two policemen were ushered into the tent by Tom. They took a seat in the front row and sat making notes. Tom looked strained, tired. The children could tell he was on edge, unusual for him. A policeman pointed to the tunnel gate. Tom appeared to be telling them how the gate could be opened and closed; he was using his arms to demonstrate that it was raised by a rope over a pulley. The policemen looked grim.

The cats were sent back to their lorry, the cage taken down and the horses entered the ring. Tom called Gustav over. The children couldn't hear what was being said but they could tell Gustav was irritated, angry even. He clearly didn't like having to explain himself to the two coppers.

The children went outside into the sunshine. Lucy was handing out invitations to her birthday party, which was on Saturday. There was to be an entertainer, a magician. It sounded great fun. Despite the troubles at the show, the children were looking forward to it.

It had to be the hottest day of the summer so far. It was now two o'clock and they were baking. 'Let's go for a swim,' suggested Laurent. The kids nodded their heads in agreement and ran to get their things. The school kids were lent bits of costumes so they wouldn't be left out. The children enjoyed being at the beach. They liked splashing in the cold water; it gave them welcome relief from the heat of the day.

When they got back to the camp, the circus folk had gathered outside the gaffer's caravan; it was too hot for them to assemble in the tent. The gaffer announced that the circus was as good as sold out for the last three weeks of the stand, just a few tickets not taken – but they were selling seats all the time. This was great news and when people were told that Chaos would make a full recovery, their spirits were lifted further. Tom then spoke. The police had said the show was safe to proceed but he said he shouldn't have to remind anyone that there was someone hard at work to ruin the circus. Yes, his tricks had backfired this time: it seemed like there really was no such thing as bad publicity – the punters wanted to see a show where danger lurked. But, nevertheless, they had to be vigilant. Who knows what might happen in the next three weeks?

At the end of the meeting, Sasha was presented with a bouquet of flowers and the circus folk gave her a round of applause. She cried. Circus people really were kind to one another. They knew Sasha was hurting inside. She had lost her beloved Tracey, but there was a tough realism to the men and women who made up the circus. They had always known of the dangers that they faced, night after night; to the public it all looked "in control", polished, but one slip and things could go badly wrong, they knew that – had always known that. They went back to their caravans that night pleased that Templeton's Circus was so popular with the people of Torquay; but at the back of their minds was a niggling thought. What would happen next in this six-week stand that had been so eventful? Even if someone had told them what lay ahead, they would not have believed them, for things were far from over...

Fourteen

Escape

The school children didn't make it to the circus ground in the early part of the week: Pete had family to stay; Lucy was away for a couple of days; Clive was unwell; and Annie went shopping with her mum for new school uniform and stuff. On Thursday, they all made it to the ground for the evening show. It felt good to be reunited. The circus folk were buzzing. It had been a week of packed performances and the gaffer had hinted of a big bonus for everyone. Sasha was talking of a Christmas holiday back to Slovakia. She wanted to buy a lion to replace Tracey. There was even talk of buying some leopards. Gustav stayed quiet. He didn't seem keen to spend any money. 'We need it,' he grumbled. 'We can't afford to spare it.'

'Nonsense,' replied Sasha, clearly irritated by her husband.

The performance went well. The crowd showed their appreciation by clapping hard. After the show, the children stood in the zoo, enjoying the summer warmth.

It had been a fantastic summer of weather. The ground was brown, parched, for there had been no rain for weeks. The children were as brown as berries. In their shorts, they were so relaxed it hurt. No school, it seemed like a lifetime since they were there.

Suddenly, there was a shout, a commotion. They strained their eyes. It had come from the direction of the bear lorry. What could they see? In the dusk, they could make out that a cage door was open. That was odd. The show was long since over. What did it mean? They ran towards the wagon. Tom was there, looking worried. 'One of the bears is loose,' he shouted. The children stood watching him, in disbelief. How could a bear be loose?

'Send for Alexei,' cried Laurent. The bears were shown by two brothers, Alexei and Gregory.

Alexei came running. 'Where iz Bella?' he screamed, staring at the empty cage. No-one knew what to say.

'Let's split up,' commanded Tom. 'She can't have got far.'

The gaffer arrived and quickly divided the assembled group into three parties. Tom's group was to go out on to the main road. Sasha's was to search the zoo. Elena's party was to comb the big top. The school children were in Tom's group. They scurried out to the road side, all the while scanning the undersides of the caravans that they were passing, eyes on stalks seeking the missing mammal. The circus folk knew that this was no joke. Bears could be dangerous, unpredictable. A frightened one could cause real havoc. And, the authorities? Well they would come down hard on a circus that had already seen someone injured with *public* safety now seemingly at risk.

They reached the road. Which way to go, left or right? They looked in both directions, to the right – nothing – just an empty street. To the left, there was something in the distance; they could just make it out – a policeman, scratching his head, his hand on his hip. They opted to go left; they were met by a strange sight. There was a bicycle, upended in a bush and there sitting on the ground, a man, dazed – looking shocked. *Bella had come this way.* The man was incoherent, mumbling. He was pale, almost green looking – was he about to be sick? The policeman was looking round. 'A large dog,' he questioned. 'You were startled by a large dog?'

'No, not a dog,' insisted the man, straining to make himself understood. 'It was big, yes, but more like a bear!'

'Don't be so ridiculous,' said the policeman, who suddenly became conscious that he was surrounded by a group of curious on-lookers.

'This way,' hissed Tom. The man was pointing down the street, and the children realised that Tom wanted them to follow him. They set off, leaving the policeman to argue with the sitting man. 'She may have headed in this direction,' said the ringmaster. 'You kids take that side of the road and Sasha and I will take this.' They spread out.

They hurried on about three hundred yards and came across a telephone box. Inside were a squashed family of four: Mum, Dad and two children, who were peering out from underneath their parents' coats. They looked like had been shoehorned into the tiny space. The dad was holding on to the door, pulling it shut, his knuckles white with the effort. Tom knocked on the window. The whole family jumped out of their skins. 'Look out,' cried the dad through the glass door. 'There's an animal on the loose. Take shelter somewhere and, before you ask, there's no room in here!' The family, packed like sardines in a can, looked fearful.

'Which way did it go?' demanded Sasha. The family pointed as one in the direction of a nearby housing estate. The circus friends ran in its direction. They passed a bus stop shelter. They spied the heads of a couple poking up at waist height, peering out through the glass. Tom stepped into the shelter. A teenage couple were crouching down, looking petrified.

'Did you see it?' asked the boy. 'A fully-grown bear came lumbering down the street. We couldn't believe what we were seeing at first. We need the police. Someone should shoot it!'

The children's hearts sank. The last thing they all needed was a police marksman taking aim at Bella, asking questions later, firing first. 'Which way did she go?' asked Tom. The pair pointed towards a thicket of trees. The gang ran towards it. They emerged from the copse onto a shopping parade. The lit shop windows illuminated the pavement; there was a fish and chip shop and an off-licence. Inside each shop stood a crowd of people, their faces pressed up against the windows, their breaths busy steaming the glass. 'That way,' mouthed the people in unison, pointing as one.

The circus party ran in the direction that they signalled. They turned into a blind alley. At the far end were some garages. 'Careful,' said Tom. 'We don't want to startle her. We'll wait here. Laurent and Sasha, run back and get Alexei. We'll need him. If Bella is here, she's trapped. We'll wait.' Laurent and Sasha sped off.

The minutes ticked by. Tom and the children tried to breathe quietly. They didn't speak. They didn't want to make any noise that might spook the bear. After what seemed like hours, they could hear approaching hushed voices. It was Alexei, Laurent and Sasha, carrying a huge net between them. 'Have you seen her?' whispered Alexei. Tom shook his head.

'But there's no other way out, she must be in one of the garages. Two have their doors up. What will you do?'

'I've bought some meat,' indicated Alexei, shaking a small bag. 'It may tempt her out.'

Getting down on his hands and knees, he crawled in the direction of the first garage. He began to make small grunting noises. If it hadn't been so serious, it would have appeared quite funny. Nothing, no response.

He stood up and moved to the other garage. Again, getting down on all fours, he shuffled forward. He began to grunt and, this time, there was an answer: a low murmur, a kind of snuffling. He gently tossed some meat into the open space, which was lit only by a nearby streetlamp. He signalled for Tom and Sasha to move forward with the net. They did so, slowly. Then suddenly, Bella emerged, blinking as she moved into the light. 'Now,' motioned Alexei. Deftly, Tom and Sasha jettisoned the net, which fell neatly over Bella. She stirred for a second but then squatted down on her haunches, tucking into the meat titbits that Alexei had thrown. The children stared at the bear. She seemed happy enough to have been captured. There was no sign of any distress for she was wolfing the meat down. Alexei was talking to her all the while, using a smooth voice; a bit like someone pouring treacle onto a pudding, thought Pete – his words were relaxing, calming, peaceful.

There was the sound of an engine. It was the bear's wagon, driven by Gregory. He manoeuvred it into the space, the headlamps illuminated all before it. For the first time, the children could see the bear clearly underneath the net. She appeared quite unharmed by her adventure. She looked bigger than ever, here, out of her normal surroundings. Gregory had brought a section of ring tunnel with him. They set about erecting it and then expertly pulled its end underneath the net that had trapped the bear. From there, they gently coaxed Bella down the tunnel and into the waiting wagon – job done!

Relieved, the children walked back with Tom and Sasha to the circus ground. They passed the phone box, which was now empty; either the family had grown braver or fed up with waiting inside and had decided to take their chances. At the top of the road, by the bush, there was no sign of the cyclist or the policeman. The children were left to wonder what had happened to the rider who had been so rudely interrupted on his way to somewhere or other.

Back at the camp, a crowd had gathered around the bear wagon, which was now parked back in its spot. The cage sides were opened and now there were once again *two* bears inside. The gaffer was there. He looked tense. A police car silently drew up. Out clambered two officers who made a beeline for the beleaguered circus boss and disappeared into his caravan. The circus folk were grumbling. They knew this was once again serious for the show. What if the bear had attacked someone?

Tom tried to quieten the crowd down. 'Being difficult,' he proclaimed with an air of authority, 'will only make matters worse.' There was the bang of a door closing and the assembled crowd looked up. The two officers had come out from the gaffer's caravan and were making their way to Alexei's and Gregory's door. They disappeared inside the trainers' caravan and soon heated voices could be heard. The four of them came out of the caravan and descended upon the cage wagon – inspecting the door, pulling it hard, looking to see if it could be opened easily. It couldn't. Well of course, it couldn't – the children knew that. All the animals' cages were locked and then locked again in order to prevent any mishaps.

After a quarter of an hour or so, the policemen made their way back to the gaffer's caravan. The crowd jeered them.

The suspense was killing the children. And then, the two officers were back in their car and gone. The gaffer reappeared. 'The police are satisfied that it couldn't have been carelessness. Someone deliberately unbolted the cage door and released Bella. It would have had to be someone who knew where Alexei and Gregory kept the keys in their caravan – the police refuse to rule out that it might have been Alexei or Gregory themselves.'

The crowd booed in derision; they knew neither brother would have released one of their animals – the bear could have been shot if the circus posse had not found it first. 'There's nothing more to be done tonight,' announced the gaffer. 'Go to bed, get some sleep. There will be time enough in the morning to talk further. Staff meeting at eleven, after morning practice.'

The crowd dispersed into the night, like steam from hot soup. The school kids bade their farewells and headed for home. What a day!

Tomorrow was Friday. Another day of sold out shows, at two thirty and seven thirty.

The next morning after practice, the performers and ring hands gathered to listen to the gaffer and Tom. The police were happy to allow the shows to go ahead but there would be a bobby at the main gate for the rest of the circus' stay. Some of the circus folk were pleased to hear this; they were worried about what might happen next. Others were less keen. They didn't trust the police and didn't want them on their doorstep each day.

'It was tough luck,' said the gaffer. 'It was out of their hands. It was either have a policeman at the gate or be shut down.' That was the last thing that they wanted. But, thought the children, that did seem to be what someone stood in that tent wanted. But who could it be? They seemed no nearer to discovering the identity of "the enemy within".

Fifteen

Cruelty Uncovered

The children were spellbound, watching the bears. It was late morning. They really were two gorgeous animals. Gregory, one of the two brothers who showed them, came over. He was wanting to clean the cage. He slid back the partition that divided the cage and shouted at Romeo, the male, to go into Bella's half of the wagon. Romeo didn't want to move. He was comfortable in the morning sunshine: why should he change compartment? Gregory quickly glanced over his shoulder, then he took a large pole and shoved it hard into Romeo's side. The bear groaned and lumbered to his feet, moving reluctantly into the adjoining section.

The watching school children winced. Shocked, they looked round at one another. They couldn't believe what they had just witnessed. They had seen no signs of animal cruelty in the show: Sasha, Manu, Gustav, they all seemed to treat their animals well. 'Come away,' urged Laurent.

'Whooa!' said Pete. 'Did you see what he just did?"

'The Popov brothers are rough with their animals,' admitted Yolanda, then added, in a rather matter-of-fact way: 'Not all trainers are kind.'

But Pete wouldn't let it rest. 'That's what it said in *The Gazette* article. The bears were beaten. Are they?'

'Like the lady says,' said Laurent, pulling his friend by the arm, 'some can be rough with their animals.'

The children moved away. Gregory had seemed oblivious to their presence, as if they didn't exist. They were just children, they guessed; the trainer obviously didn't worry about what kids saw. 'Does the gaffer know?' asked Lucy.

'Yes,' said Natalie, 'but the brothers are cheap to hire. He keeps them on because of that.'

The school children went quiet. They were disappointed. The circus life had seemed one of good-naturedness and glamour – exciting, real, but above all honest.

They had lunch outside. Things were out of kilter. For the first time, the school children were uneasy. This was something they had to challenge; they couldn't just let it go... wouldn't just let it go!

That afternoon, they went to watch the two brothers present their bears in the show. Behind the curtain they were stern with the two animals, keeping them on a tight rein. The bears wore muzzles and the brothers each had a whip. The school children hadn't paid much attention to the Russians before. There had been so much to see at the circus. But now they were focussed on the two men. They dissected their every move as they prepared for their turn. As they entered the ring, they were all smiles, teeth shining with fixed grins. They made a fuss of the two creatures, rubbed their backs, playfully kissed them. The bears had a full routine. They first climbed a ladder to go down a slide. Then they mounted a bicycle to career around the ring. Next, they balanced upon balls to make their way from one side of the ring to another. Finally, they donned boxing gloves and play fought Gregory, whilst Alexei watched on. The crowd loved them. Pete couldn't help but feel a little uncomfortable. They were such lovely animals but rather than marvel at them, the crowd seemed to be laughing. It seemed such a shame. They were too grand to be laughed at – too regal.

As soon as they were on the other side of the curtains, their act complete, Gregory and Alexei's broad grins evaporated. They reverted to their sullen looks and tugged at the animals to make them go all the quicker back to their wagon. The bears were chased back up into their cage.

The children stood round the wagon, watching the two beasts. They felt sorry for them. It was another hot evening and they needed a drink. There was nothing in their bowls. 'Let's water them,' said Laurent. They made their way to the main tap and filled a bucket. They tipped water into the bears' drinking trough and the animals lapped it up eagerly. The children flopped down onto the grass. They had some sandwiches to eat for tea and they set about them. They were hungry.

'This is all wrong,' said Pete, angrily. 'They shouldn't be able to treat these creatures in this way; it's simply not fair.'

Yolanda looked perplexed. 'As my grandmother would say,' she said, 'one rotten apple does not the pie spoil.' The school kids frowned. What did she mean exactly?

Laurent spoke up. 'There are good parents, there are bad parents; some smack their children, others do not. In the same way, we have some trainers who are good to their animals, some who are less good.'

Pete was unconvinced. 'That's not good enough,' he said. 'If a child is naughty, they may get a smack. My mum smacks me. But naughty children don't get hit with a pole in the belly.'

Laurent shrugged. 'I wish it wasn't this way, but we have some bad men in the circus. That is life, we cannot change it.'

'It takes all sorts to make a world,' said Clive suddenly; he had heard his parents say this on many an occasion.

Time was getting on. Alexei and Gregory came running to the wagon and began to prepare for the evening performance. It would soon be the bears' turn to perform again. Alexei led Bella down the ramp from her cage; Gregory took charge of Romeo. Bella was being difficult for she was tired from the afternoon heat. She reared up. Alexei pulled her down forcibly by her lead and whacked her hard on the nose with the end of a stick that he was carrying. Pete was incensed. Laurent stepped in between him and the trainers. 'Leave it,' he hissed.'

'What do you children want?' shouted Gregory, as if he was seeing the children for the very first time. 'Clear off back to your caravans and play with your dolls, stay away from adult business.'

The two men wandered off towards the big top, their bears on leads. The children followed at a distance. Behind the curtains, stood the two men. The bears' leads were wrapped tightly round their fists. The band struck up the act's music, a Russian tune, and the two men's fixed smiles appeared again as they ran into the ring. They again made a fuss of their animals. Pete, who stood watching from the wings, thought how much the crowd must think the trainers loved the animals – if only they knew the sordid truth.

The children followed the two trainers back to the wagon; Pete insisted. Bella was straining at her leash. Gregory aimed a kick at her bottom. She grunted in discomfort and sprinted up the ramp into her den. The school children looked at one another. 'Let's find the gaffer,' said Pete.

'No, let's not,' said Laurent. 'He won't want to listen to kids.'

'That's where you're wrong,' said Pete and the other school kids nodded in unison. Natalie was impressed. Pete seemed so grown-up, so handsome. The children found the gaffer at the back of the tent, smoking.

'Hi, kids,' he said, seeming genuinely pleased to see them. Pete drew in a deep breath and spoke ten to the dozen.

'You have a pair of bullies on this show,' he said. 'The Popov brothers are mean to their animals, who mean them no harm.'

'There are many ways to skin a cat, kid,' the gaffer said. He didn't look over concerned. He was talking to a group of children at the end of the day – confident kids, by the looks of it, especially this Pete boy, but kids nevertheless.

'If you don't sort them out,' said Pete, 'we will tell the papers what we've seen here today. It's downright cruel.'

The gaffer flicked the butt of his cigarette nonchalantly into the air and stubbing it out with his heel, turned to face the children square on. 'That sounds like a threat,' he barked, looking none too pleased.

Laurent and Yolanda pulled at Pete's arm. 'Leave it,' they said.

'You would do well to listen to your friends,' said the gaffer. 'This is my show and I'll run it as I see fit.'

'If you don't sort them out,' argued Pete, 'I will be talking to my parents and we will contact *The Gazette* tomorrow to let them know what is going on.'

The circus boss looked straight at the boy. He was just a child. But the circus could not afford any more damaging headlines. Pete knew it, more importantly, the gaffer knew it.

'I'll speak to the Popovs,' he said, suddenly changing tack, dancing to Pete's tune. 'Sure, I will. This is my circus, can't have my performers upsetting a member of the public.' With that he strode off. The kids gathered around Pete.

'You were magnificent,' said Timmy. 'Bravissimo!'

Natalie squeezed his hand; she hated the Popovs.

The children flopped down outside the big top. The show was coming to an end. Tom walked past, on his way into the tent to wrap things up. 'Hi, kids,' he said. 'Having fun?'

Laurent spoke up. 'We've just been putting right something that was wrong.'

'Great,' said Tom, looking bemused. 'Like to hear about things being put right,' he said, with a wry smile that puzzled the children.

Natalie and Yolanda said goodnight and headed for their caravan. Lucy and Annie were also calling it a day. This just left the five boys lying out in the evening warmth. It was eight o'clock or thereabouts. 'So,' said Timmy, 'what's it like to be in love, Pete?'

Pete laughed. 'Great,' he said. 'Who knows, at this rate, I may join the show.' The boys laughed, all but Laurent. Timmy spied the French boy's discomfort.

'Come on, Laurent,' he said. 'You can't blame Pete for the fact that Natalie chose him over you.' Timmy was wanting a reaction. He was being mischievous.

Laurent knew it. He looked peeved but then broke into a smile. 'Pete's won the first round,' he said, 'but in a couple of weeks' time the show will be on the move. Natalie will be looking for a new boyfriend and I'll be there and Mr Pete will be ancient history.'

The circus boys laughed. Laurent had turned the tables. Pete looked to his friend Clive for help but there was nothing Clive could say. It was true. The circus folk were always on the move. *Here today, gone tomorrow.* True they had stayed longer here in Torquay but the day was coming when they would be off. Laurent would be able to chat up Natalie and there was nothing his friend, Pete, could do about it. Pete laughed. But the boys could tell he didn't find the situation funny – not at all.

There was suddenly a loud commotion from the Popovs' caravan. The gaffer was walking backwards down the steps of their caravan. He was shouting. The two Russians were yelling back and making rude gestures with their arms. 'Oh, no,' said Laurent. 'Things haven't gone well.'

'This is my circus,' said the gaffer, 'and in my circus things are done my way, in only my way!'

The school boys jumped up. 'We'd better be off,' they said. 'See you in the morning.' They made their way to the bus stop. Where was the bus? They had to be in by nine, or there would be trouble. With a loud bang from its exhaust, a wagon farted its way onto the road. It passed the two boys and they spied the two Popov brothers in the cab. The bear wagon was pulling the brothers' caravan along, like a dog straining at a lead.

'Wow,' said Clive. 'Looks like the gaffer has thrown them out. Well done, mate, you sure sorted them!'

Pete was quiet. 'I didn't though, did I?' he said. 'They are off with their bears – they'll find another circus where they will go on mistreating them. I wanted the gaffer to make them stop, change their ways, not sling them out. Who is going to be looking out for those bears now?'

The bus drew up and the two boys clambered aboard. 'Maybe they will act differently now,' said Clive, taking a seat, 'now that the gaffer has called their bluff.'

'Maybe,' said Pete. But just as he couldn't be sure Natalie wouldn't look for another boyfriend when the show moved on, he couldn't be sure either that the Popov brothers would turn over a new leaf at their next show. Not all circus folk were good people, it seemed.

Sixteen

Secret Out

Saturday promised to be a better day. There were two shows and Lucy's party to look forward to. Pete was angling for another kiss from Natalie. He'd had only one since the school disco. He wasn't sure if Natalie had gone cold on him. He hoped not. There were only two weeks remaining before the end of the summer season. Then the circus would move, taking Natalie with it, leaving Pete behind, back to square one, without a girlfriend. They had talked about staying an item, writing to one another but it was hard to see how it would work. The circus was always on the move. How would he know where to send letters to? She could always write to him, she had said. But that seemed like one way traffic to Pete. Next year, the circus might return to Torquay but that was only a "might" – nothing was certain in the circus world. Pete found it depressing to think about. He had waited a long time to get his first girlfriend, now she was disappearing and there was nothing he could do about it.

He was a kid, after all; he couldn't just up and join the circus, it didn't work like that.

There was the usual hustle and bustle in the zoo during the morning. All the kids were there to watch what went on. Each act practised every morning; the children helped walk the elephants into the ring, then the horses. Pete asked Natalie how the trainers always made sure that the animals didn't poo during their act. 'They're trained "to go" before,' she replied. 'We hold a shovel of manure in front of the horse's nose and they soon get the message. Elephants stand with one leg on a pedestal; they know then to do their business.' There were always new things to learn in the circus.

Practice was important to the circus folk. They used it to maintain their skills, keep themselves sharp and it was a time that some performers would try out new things, which might make their way into their act at a later date.

The children especially liked watching the trapeze artists practise – Kristabel, Oleg, Aaron and Pieter. They flew through the air at literally breakneck speed; all the time shouting to one another to ensure that their act was timed to perfection. 'It was all in the timing,' said Natalie, who longed to perform on the rope one day, high up in the roof of the big top. Her parents had an aerial act and they trained her and Yolanda each morning on the floor, to make their bodies supple and ready for the day when they would be suspended from on high.

Yolanda explained the flying trapeze act to them. There was a catcher: he had to be strong with great hands. He would wrap his knees round a bar swinging down from one side of the big top's ceiling and hang upside down, his arms dangling down like those of a monkey. The flier had to put their trust in those hands; if they weren't there to catch him, he could fall to his death. The flier would begin to swing on his bar, swinging from the opposite side, his hands wrapped tightly over it, legs hanging loose; he would wait for the moment when the catcher signalled with a shout that he was ready for him. At the right moment, when they were both swinging through the air in unison, the flier would let go of his bar and fly through the air to the catcher. *Pure poetry in motion*, thought Clive. There was a net below but that would not be enough necessarily to save you, should you fall. Fliers had been known to bounce off the net and land on the ring floor – break their backs, or worse.

The children sat watching the fliers. 'How long have they been with your show?' asked Pete.

'Just this year,' replied Yolanda. 'They are the only new act this year; the rest of us have been here for some time.' The children were all thinking the same thing. If it wasn't Demetrius or Chaos, could it be one of the fliers? It stood to reason that it was more likely to be a newcomer.

'What do you know about them?' asked Pete.

Laurent pulled a face. 'Not much, they keep themselves to themselves.'

'The catcher, Pieter, has a nasty temper,' interjected Natalie.

Pieter was huge and strong and his muscles were obviously a source of great pride to him. He wore the tightest of costumes. When they had first arrived, explained Natalie, they had insisted they had star billing, rather than any of the animal acts. But the gaffer wouldn't give in. The animals he had said were the stars of our show. The children wondered. *Could Pieter be the enemy within, but why would he have done these things? He might be jealous of the animals' star billing but it didn't seem sufficient motive for trying to bring Templeton's Circus to its knees.*

They decided to do some digging. 'Let's ask Tom,' said Annie. The others nodded. Tom was outside his caravan, washing before the afternoon show.

'Pieter,' he puzzled. 'Yes he has a temper sure enough. Look,' he said. 'I've been giving the matter some thought too. It seems to me we have three main suspects: Pieter was on my list too for he created a terrible stink when the gaffer refused to give him top billing; he hates the animal acts, thinks they take the attention away from his fliers; he thinks we should be giving the punters a new circus, where we celebrate human skill and not an animal show.' Natalie caught Pete's eye; they both thought the same thing as the catcher but for a different reason; they wanted to see all human shows because of their concern for the animals' welfare. 'Then there's Elena,' went on Tom, 'I've never trusted her.' The children were stunned: beautiful Elena. The children hadn't imagined for a moment that the enemy might be a woman.

'But, the person who sabotaged the posters was a man,' chipped in Pete. This was true. The shopkeepers had all agreed.

Tom shrugged. 'Elena is moving on at the end of this season. She wanted more money but the gaffer refused to increase her wages. She is bitter. She doesn't have another circus to go to yet and the gaffer is refusing to recommend her to other shows; says she is greedy. She is a suspect for me. Everyone thinks that we are dealing with a man but she could easily have paid a man to do the rounds of the shops for her, getting the posters sabotaged. Finally,' said Tom, looking awkward... Well maybe it's best if I don't say...' His voice trailed off.

'Go on,' urged the children as one. 'Who is it? Who else do you suspect?'

'Well,' said Tom, 'you won't like it, Timmy and Olaf, but I half suspect your old man, Gustav.' The two boys went red.

'You've got to be joking,' said Timmy. 'Our dad would never do anything like that.' The other children felt embarrassed for the two boys.

'Gustav was perfectly placed to let Tracey into the ring cage when the lights were out,' argued Tom. 'Whoever lifted the tunnel gate knew how to do it very well indeed, they were working in the dark, remember.'

'Nevertheless,' said Olaf, coming to his father's defence, 'he wouldn't have done any of it. He's no reason to.'

Tom's shoulders shot up in a defiant shrug. 'I said you wouldn't like it,' he answered.

The children melted away, leaving Tom to finish his wash in peace. The children rallied round the two boys. 'No way,' said Pete. 'Besides, Gustav lost a lioness through it. Why would he have done that?' The other children nodded in agreement.

'Elena or Pieter then,' said Annie.

'Yes one of the two, perhaps,' said Olaf.

'Or maybe they're working together,' said Natalie. The children stopped in their tracks. They hadn't considered before that there could be more than one person acting against the show. 'That would explain why the person who visited the shops was a man; that could have been Pieter.'

'Are they friends?' asked Lucy.

'No,' replied Laurent. 'Quite the opposite, they're rivals. They each perform in the air; they want to be the best up there. The fliers don't speak to Elena because she is the competition.' The children were disappointed. There went their theory.

'Let's spend the afternoon watching them,' said Peter. 'See what they get up to.' The children split up. They had agreed to dot themselves about the camps in twos and a three, to try and look inconspicuous; to spot Pieter and Elena, and to see what they got up to.

The afternoon wore on. It was so hot. Laurent and Lucy were sitting outside the elephant tent. They were reading, or at least, pretending to read. From their vantage point they could see the fliers' caravan, who came down the steps mid-afternoon, dressed for their act and made their way into the big top. The children looked at their watches. It was two thirty. 'They'll be about twenty minutes,' calculated Laurent. Sure enough, twenty minutes later the four acrobats came laughing and joking out of the tent, shooting up the steps to their caravans. Minutes later, changed, Pieter came down the steps and with his hands in his pockets, made his way whistling round the tent. The children rose to follow him.

Meanwhile, Pete, Annie and Yolanda were watching Elena's caravan. It was a poky little thing, parked right round the back of the show. There was no sign of Elena. She would be in the big top, performing. Then they spied her, waltzing her way back through the field after her spot in the ring. They ducked down out of sight behind a wagon – more waiting. Would she ever come out? Pete fell asleep in the afternoon sun. Annie and Yolanda were about to follow suit when they were startled by the sound of a caravan door shutting. It was Elena, who was on the move. Pete looked at his watch. It was just coming up to three o'clock. They jumped up and skirted round the vehicles, keeping Elena in their sights. They saw her leave the site by the main gate, saying 'Hello,' to the copper who was standing sentry there. She headed off to the right.

Laurent and Lucy were following Pieter. He had passed through the gate moments earlier, nodding in the direction of the policeman, and heading to the left. They followed him to the end of the road, where he turned right then right again. He kept looking over his shoulder as if he knew he was being followed. *But he couldn't know, could he?* The children were staying well back, keeping close to the trees that lined the avenue. They watched him carefully. He turned sharply left and disappeared into a posh looking restaurant. They crossed the road, and hid in a bus shelter opposite. They crouched down behind the grey panels. Hidden from view, they peered up and out through the glass partition. They could not see Pieter, who must have taken a seat at the back.

Meanwhile, Pete, Annie and Yolanda had followed Elena. She had hurried at a fair old pace in the opposite direction to Pieter. But, then she turned left and then left again. She too kept glancing over her shoulder. It was suspicious. Maybe she didn't want to be followed.

Back at the bus shelter, Laurent and Lucy suddenly saw Elena. They almost burst with excitement. Had they been right all along? Were the two in cahoots? Was Elena coming to meet Pieter? They watched Elena; they were willing her to enter the restaurant. She stood and looked round, then as quick as a flash she darted inside. Laurent punched the air, 'Gotcha,' he hissed, much to the amusement of an old lady who was now waiting inside the bus shelter. Suddenly the two children saw Pete, Annie and Yolanda come into view. The children stopped outside of the restaurant then hurried in the direction of the bus shelter. What a surprise they got when they dived in. There, crouching on the floor, were Laurent and Lucy.

'Quick get down,' urged Laurent. 'They might see you.'

'Who do you mean, "they"?' demanded Pete, bemused.

'Pieter and Elena, they're both in the restaurant.'

The children each explained how they had followed their suspect. The old lady sat listening, entranced; she hadn't expected such entertainment to come in the middle of her lazy afternoon. The children's brains raced on overtime. They could hardly get their words out, they were so excited. Had they discovered at long last who had spoilt the posters? Cut the microphone and lights in the afternoon performance? Let Tracey into the cage to attack Chaos, and let Bella loose? They so wished they could tell Tom and the others what they had discovered.

It was hot in the shelter and they loosened their clothing. They wished they had drinks but there was nothing. It made them mad to think that all the while, Pieter and Elena were opposite in a restaurant, eating and drinking, planning their next move. A bus drew up. People got off, stepping round the five children, wondering what on earth was going on. Then came another. More passengers alighted. All went quiet. Suddenly, the children watching through the glass saw the restaurant door open. Out stepped Pieter and Elena. Nothing had prepared the children for what happened next. For, as they emerged into the sunshine, the two performers were "holding hands". They stood outside the restaurant and kissed. They looked so relaxed and happy.

The children looked at one another, flabbergasted. The reason the two performers had not wanted to be followed was not because they were plotting against the show; the reason was more simple than that – they were in love – a secret romance; one that they had to keep quiet from the other fliers, who saw Elena as a rival. The old lady sitting in the shelter, who had purposely missed her bus twice, so much was she enjoying the action, began to laugh out loud. The children could not help but join in. They were soon holding their sides, creased up with giggles. What fools they had been!

Seventeen

Fondue

Lucy's party started with a bang. The Johnson twins from Class 4F arrived. They were always good for a laugh. They had brought an LP by Mud, "Mud Rock". The children enjoyed dancing to "Tiger Feet", doing the actions: thumbs in their belts, criss-crossing their feet. They enjoyed eating Smith's Cheese 'n' Onion crisps and drinking Coke – it was after all "the real thing", they chorused. Pete was watching Natalie. *Would she dance with him?* He hoped so.

The nine children were sitting in the garden. 'I suppose that Elena and Pieter could still be the "enemy"?' ventured Lucy. 'Just because they are in *lurve*, doesn't mean they aren't up to no good.' The others weren't buying it. The two aerial performers had looked so carefree, so happy; they hadn't looked like two people who were scheming and full of mischief. The schools kids looked down at the grass, not wanting to catch Timmy and Olaf's gaze. They were all thinking the same thing. Could Tom be right? Could it be Gustav?

Timmy spoke up. 'We know what you're thinking,' he mumbled. 'Olaf and I have been talking. Dad hasn't been his usual self for some time – always popping off to see the gaffer or somewhere else – always moaning. He says we don't have any money. Yet, we have been raking it in these past few weeks. We're not saying it's him that we're looking for. But still…' his voice trailed off.

'He plays in the same card school as Chaos,' observed Laurent. 'I've seen him there.'

'Yes, he does play cards with Chaos, Tom and the others,' agreed Timmy. 'He never used to do that, it's just been this year.'

'Maybe he owes money, like Chaos,' suggested Laurent. *But how would destroying Templeton's Circus get him money?* The children sat and reflected.

'Does the gaffer have any competitors?' asked Annie. 'Other circuses who might want to see him ruined?' It was a thought, a real idea. The school kids looked at Laurent and the other circus kids.

'Well,' exclaimed Natalie, 'there is another show that the circus often clashes with – Billy Bright's show. Last year, we raced to get on to the same grounds before one another. And, then there was that time the Bright men ripped our posters down.' The children sat deep in thought.

Laurent was the first to speak. 'Maybe Gustav needs money and Billy Bright is providing it in return for some favours…'

Wow! This could be it. Maybe Bright could be behind the whole thing. It made perfect sense.

'If Dad owes money, Chaos would know,' said Olaf suddenly. The children were interrupted by Joanne Dawson, a friend of Lucy's, who came out to ask them to come back inside – they wanted to sing Happy Birthday to Lucy – her mum was ready with the cake.

The children went inside. They couldn't remember a summer as exciting as this one. There didn't seem time even for cake. Pete made a beeline for Natalie. 'Can I talk to you?' he asked, 'outside, away from the others.' The two children went outside into the garden. 'Can I have a kiss?' said Pete. Natalie smiled. She kissed him on the lips. Pete felt good. 'I'm going to miss you,' he complained, 'when you move on.'

'And I'll miss you,' she confided. 'Let's not think about it.'

Back inside the children had finished singing Happy Birthday and Lucy had blown out the candles on her cake. 'Make a wish,' said her mum. Lucy closed her eyes.

'What did you wish for?' Pete inquired.

'That we could discover who the enemy is, of course,' she whispered. They smiled at one another.

Lucy's mum called for them to be quiet. They were going to be treated to some fondue; such parties were all the rage. There was a small pot heated by a gas ring. Inside was molten chocolate. This looked like fun. There were to be two teams: the boys against the girls. You had to stab a piece of fruit with a skewer, dip it into the chocolate mixture, eat it, then run to the end of the room, turn round, run back and hand the skewer to your teammate. If you were beaten you had to do a forfeit. The team with the fewest forfeits would win.

The circus kids found themselves split: Laurent and Natalie on one team; Yolanda, Timmy and Olaf on the other. Pete and Lucy kicked off for their respective teams. Fruit dunked and swallowed, they ran to the end of the living room. Pete was first to get back. Lucy had to serve a forfeit. *Walk round the room as a chimp with a banana in his mouth might.* The next two to race were Samantha Millbank and Clive. Clive was determined not to have to serve a forfeit. His piece of fruit hardly touched the sides of his mouth. It was gone in one gulp. He was back with his skewer before Samantha had reached the far end of the living room. Samantha's forfeit was to pretend she was riding a horse over some high jumps. Clive breathed a sigh of relief; he would not have wanted to do that! The children dissolved into fits of laughter when for a forfeit, Timmy had to act as if he were a chicken with its bottom on fire.

After the game, the children got to dip more fruit, this time at a leisurely pace, into the chocolate. It was delicious. They lay out in the garden and gazed up at the stars that had begun to twinkle in the night sky. 'What do you want to do when you are all older?' asked Pete. 'You go first Natalie.'

'That's easy,' she said, 'fly the trapeze, it's all I have ever wanted to do. Laurent, how 'bout you?'

'Run my own show,' he declared, proudly. 'Be the gaffer. How about you, Pete?'

'A doctor,' he replied. The circus kids looked on. It never occurred to them to be anything outside of the circus life. That was for other folk, not them.

'I want to have the largest lion act in Europe,' said Timmy.

Olaf wasn't so sure. 'I can see a time when circuses will have to do without animals – the cranks will win one day,' he said. 'Every year, they grow stronger; there are more of them at the gate and they are louder.'

'Rubbish,' voiced Timmy. 'That day will never come.' Pete and Natalie said nothing.

For a while the children had forgotten Templeton's and its troubles. But the next day was to bring yet more surprises.

Eighteen

A Train Ride

The children gathered together at the campsite early on Sunday. There was a lot to discuss. Could Gustav be the one? Timmy and Olaf clearly didn't want to buy into the idea. Dad was Dad. Miserable sometimes, prone to disappearing for ages on end, but still Dad; he wouldn't be involved – couldn't be – Chaos could have been killed, for goodness sake. Their dad wasn't a murderer!

What to do next?

'You say he disappears from time-to-time,' repeated Pete. 'Well, where is he going?' The lion boys didn't know.

Stumped for ideas, later that morning, Timmy, Laurent and Natalie went to visit Chaos in hospital. He was on the mend. Nevertheless, his good humour seemed to be intact for he smiled when he saw the children. 'Hi, kids,' he said. 'How's tricks?' He had been moved to a different ward. He would be coming back to the circus in a few days' time. He wouldn't be able to perform to begin with, but he hoped to be back in the show before the end of September. The children were pleased for him. They told him about Bella escaping. 'Hmmn,' he said. 'Someone sure has it in for Templeton's.'

'Can we talk to you about Gustav?' asked Natalie.

'Gustav,' responded the clown. 'Sure, what do you want to know?'

'Does Dad owe money?' asked Timmy.

'A pile,' said Chaos. 'I've never seen such a run of bad luck, but he keeps coming back for more.' The clown looked awkward, like he was disclosing a secret he shouldn't be sharing.

There it was – the motive. There seemed very little else to say. The children wanted to get away and talk it over. They made their excuses and left. The children got the bus back to the camp. They met there with the others, who had been waiting for them. What had they discovered? They shared their news. No-one was pleased. This wasn't fun. They may well be close to solving the mystery, but no-one felt good about it, Gustav was Timmy and Olaf's dad. This was serious.

'What shall we do?' asked Annie. 'Timmy and Olaf, you decide, it's your dad we're talking about.'

'If it's Dad, we need to ask him,' said Timmy. 'We'll do it tomorrow, after the show. That will give us time to think what we are going to say. It's not every day you accuse your dad of being a criminal. If Dad is involved he must owe someone money and need someone to lend him some.'

'Billy Bright,' said Pete. 'Why not?'

'Where is Bright's Circus at the moment?' asked Annie. The circus kids shrugged their shoulders; they hadn't a clue.

'Tom would know,' said Laurent. 'Let's ask him.'

They found the ringmaster.

'Billy Bright's show, why do you want to know?' asked Tom.

'Just interested,' said Laurent, 'no particular reason.'

Tom looked suspicious. 'I don't know why it would interest you, but he is just up the road in Dawlish.' The children tried hard not to show their excitement, just a stone's throw away. Could it be the answer to the mystery? Away from Tom, the children could hardly contain themselves.

'Let's go to his show,' said Laurent.

'We can't,' said Pete. 'It's a train journey away. We don't have the necessary.'

'I have my birthday money,' offered Lucy. The children looked up. It was good of Lucy to step forward. How much did she have? A whole pound, it would be enough to get them to Dawlish and back. Dare they? They jumped at the chance. Lucy scurried off home with Annie. They would collect the money and meet the others at the station.

Half an hour later, the children assembled on the station platform. The next train to Dawlish was in an hour. It seemed a lifetime to wait. They bought some ice creams and sat down on a bench. The express pulled in, on its way to London. A man struggled through from the station entrance with a large suitcase. His travelling companion was outside with their taxi; they were taking it in relays to empty the taxi of their luggage and load it into the stationary train. The guard started to close the doors. Clive, oblivious to the fact that one of the two men was on the train, the other with the taxi, closed their compartment door. The boy was just trying to be helpful. The guard seeing that all the doors were shut, blew his whistle and the train pulled away. The man on the train was hanging out of the window, signalling to his friend who was now running alongside the moving train. One man was on his way to London, the other was not. Clive, realising his mistake, kept his head down. The children did laugh.

The Dawlish train pulled in at last and the children scrambled on board. It was a lovely route; the train ran along the sea wall. As they pulled into their destination, the kids jumped out. Where was the circus? They didn't have far to look. They could see the big top rising from the centre of the park that stood in the middle of the small town. They made their way in its direction. Everywhere they looked there were posters for the Bright show. It seemed to be quite a big affair. What should their next move be?

Laurent had already thought about that. He had brought a programme of the Templeton show with him. Inside was a large glossy picture of Gustav with his lions.

'I thought we might show it around, ask some of the tent hands if they have seen Gustav knocking about at the show.' It was a brilliant idea.

The children bought tickets for the zoo. It was different to the Templeton show. As well as lions, they had polar bears. The children stood and marvelled at them for they were huge, lean with fur that was tinged yellow at the ends. There was a circus hand leaning against the barrier erected to keep the punters away from the bears. Laurent showed him the programme and Gustav; he shook his head, no he hadn't seen that man at their show.

They moved onto the elephant tent. Bright had a mixed herd of African and Indian pachyderms. They stood swaying from side to side, just like the ladies back at Templeton's. The Africans were bigger than their Indian cousins. They had larger ears and straighter backs. 'I prefer the Indian ones,' remarked Lucy. 'They look more circus-ey.'

There were two stable hands chatting nearby, keeping a watchful eye on the five beasts. Laurent again showed the programme. He came back to the children. 'Nothing doing,' he said. 'Never seen Gustav before.'

The children were just a little dispirited. It had seemed like a good idea but there seemed no-one in the show that had seen the lion tamer. They asked some more people: a clown and the girl at the booking office. No luck there either. They wandered back through the zoo and turned a corner. To their surprise, they ran straight into Gregory. He was not at all pleased to see them.

'What are you doing here?' he spat viciously.

'We could ask you the same thing,' replied Pete.

'We are with the Bright show now, a much better affair than Templeton's.'

'Says you,' said Laurent.

'Are you here to make more trouble? Accusing more people of mistreating their animals, I shouldn't wonder.' The bear trainer looked really unhappy to see them. He started to shout. 'These kids are trouble,' he cried.

Hearing the commotion, a crowd began to form. One of the hands from earlier spoke up. 'They were asking questions about some other trainer. Had I seen him?' he said. Things were turning nasty. The children didn't like the look of the faces that were surrounding them.

'Come on,' urged Laurent, 'let's shoot.' They turned and ran for the gate with jeers chasing them. The children looked round and saw Popov arriving on the scene. They had got out just in time. The last thing they wanted to do was encounter both brothers at the same time.

They walked back towards the front. 'It was always a long shot,' said Lucy.

'Just because no-one recognised Gustav doesn't mean that he is not involved. What about Gregory and Popov?' said Pete. 'It's kind of suspicious that they've turned up with the Bright show.'

'Yes, but they wouldn't have set their own bear free, would they?' Lucy reminded them.

'I'm not so sure,' said Pete, his mind racing. 'They don't exactly care about their bears – if Bright had been paying them to put the Templeton show out of business, it might be something they would do.' The children went quiet. There seemed to be so many twists and turns to this adventure. Maybe the Russian brothers were behind it all.

They sat at the station and watched the waves roll in. They enjoyed sitting in the sun. 'It was really kind of you to spend your birthday money on the train fares, Lucy,' said Laurent. The others nodded in agreement. She was a brick. Their train pulled into the station and they boarded it. As the train was pulling away, Gregory and Alexei ran on to the platform, shouting. They could see the children sitting in their compartment. They ran along and banged on the carriage windows. Laurent stood up and made a rude gesture with his hands. He wasn't frightened of this pair, given that was, the train was already moving! Meanwhile, the others slid deep down in their seats, this pair of Russians really were nasty bits of work. It took them a while to gather their thoughts.

Much later, the school kids made their way home by bus. It had been a long day. Were they any closer to solving the mystery? No. And, now they had three suspects, not two – Gregory and Alexei had joined Gustav on their list.

That night, more than one of the children dreamed of being chased by the two Russian brothers.

Nineteen

Secret Out!

The following day the children headed for the beach. It was Monday, a rest day. Less than two weeks of the Torquay stand now remained. They frolicked on the sand. Pete was after another kiss with Natalie. He could still remember the last one; it had felt good. The children flopped down, tired from sunshine and sea. 'Let's not forget Bruce,' said Lucy, 'or Pieter or Elena or Gregory or Alexei.'

'No,' said Laurent. 'Gustav is our man, Tom's right.'

The children pondered. So many suspects, but why would someone want to ruin the circus? Could it be that Billy Bright was paying someone? They went back in the water and played with the ball. At the back of their minds was the thought that the summer was coming to an end. The children didn't want to think about it, they were enjoying themselves so. They came back out and lay down on the sand. The sun beat down.

'What's your earliest memory of the circus?' asked Lucy. The circus children thought.

'I can remember being very young,' said Timmy, 'and Mamma putting a lion cub in my playpen. Its teeth were sharp. I could have only been about three.'

'How 'bout you, Natalie?' asked Pete.

'Toni took me to the top of the tent when I was no more than six,' she answered. 'I stood at the top of the tent looking down. I knew then that I wanted to be alive in the air, high up. Everything seemed so small from there, like toy town.'

The school kids went quiet. Their lives seemed so mundane in comparison. Pete's earliest memory was of his first day at school: his mum had given him a Milky Way for break time. It was hardly in the same league as being given a lion cub as a playmate. He didn't dare mention it.

'Do you ever wish you had an ordinary life?' said Pete. 'Isn't it tiring always being on the move, in all weathers?'

'It's what we're used to,' replied Natalie. 'Sometimes, I look at people in their neat, tidy homes and imagine what that would be like? But circus is in our blood, it's what we do.'

The school kids sighed. They were envious of the circus children, whose lives were so very glamorous.

When they got back to the campsite, there were new arrivals: Pepe and Pablo, two Spanish clowns, who were assisted by a third, white-faced, clown, who turned out to be Pepe's wife, Lucinda. Dark skinned, the three Spaniards had broad toothy smiles and they wore the most colourful clothes. The three Spaniards were to stand in for Chaos till he was able to come back to the show.

The circus performers gathered in the big top to watch the newcomers run through their routine; it was a tradition for the circus folk to see any new act before an audience. The circus was full of such traditions and superstitions too – the circus folk didn't like the colour green or the number thirteen.

The clowns' act was funny. The assembled crowd enjoyed it. It was different to Chaos' routine, having two main parts. The first was what Pete called "toilet humour". Pepe started by playing a piccolo, a loud tuneful toot came from the instrument: toot, toot, toot, toot then Pablo came running up and snatched the piccolo off him; he blew through the instrument, only for a loud rude noise to play through one of the speakers. There were loud guffaws of laughter. There followed more "farting" around, quite literally; explosions of powder shooting from Pepe's bottom with every rude sound that was made. Both clowns' trousers fell down at different points, revealing legs that had tights on with large black plastic hairs protruding from skinny legs. It was Lucinda's job to keep them in order. She kept ordering them from the tent but they came up with ways to avoid taking their leave.

The second half of the act comprised the three clowns making music, lots of it – playing a trumpet, a saxophone and an accordion. This part of the act seemed to go on for ages. Pablo, Pepe and Lucinda were very proud of their musical abilities. They were talented and wanted the whole world to know it.

The next day, Tuesday, the schoolchildren teamed up with their circus pals before the two thirty show. Had

Timmy and Olaf decided to approach their dad? Yes. They had decided to ask him outright. *Was he behind it all?* Timmy couldn't believe that his dad would have done anything that would have seen one of his lions dead. But the others weren't so sure. Now they thought about it Gustav seemed uptight all the time, always on edge.

'Shall we do some busking?' asked Laurent with a cheeky grin. The circus children smiled; the school kids looked confused. Busking. What did they mean? 'Come on,' said Laurent. The children followed him to his caravan. He disappeared inside, only to reappear seconds later with a saxophone and a portable tape player.

'I didn't know you could play the sax,' said Pete.

'I can't,' said Laurent with a wink. 'But the punters don't need to know that, do they?'

The circus kids led the way to the front of the big top where a large queue had formed. Laurent approached it. He pressed the play button and music started to play. He ran his fingers deftly over the saxophone keys. The punters thought the tape was only playing backing music, and Laurent was playing along live on the saxophone. Little did they know that all the music they were hearing was in fact coming from the tape recording. People who were waiting began to throw coins in a cap that Natalie had placed in front of Laurent. Suddenly Tom Parker appeared.

'Quick,' said Yolanda, stopping the tape, 'scarper.' The children dashed off out of reach of the laughing ringmaster, as quick as rats deserting a sinking ship.

'Thirty-two pence,' counted Laurent. It was enough to buy them ice creams and have some change. The school kids were amazed; the brass neck of these circus children, they knew no shame! It had been funny though.

The five o'clock show was packed. The children were passed in by Tom, who was still laughing about their little stunt outside. 'Kids,' he chuckled, with a little shrug of the shoulders. The children sat in the back row. There was no Sasha, and Gustav called upon Timmy and Olaf to help out the back with the cats. Gustav didn't know where Sasha was. The cats seemed edgy, bad tempered even. Perhaps Sasha's absence was disturbing them. The children clapped the cats but they could not get off their minds that the enemy might be unmasked that very evening.

Next came the new clowns. The children liked their jokes but the adults in the audience were left quite cold, like chicken in a fridge. The grown-ups didn't find the bottom humour funny, but they enjoyed the music, which the children in turn found boring – it went on and on and on. The gaffer was displeased. The show was missing Chaos: this "continental" style of humour was not playing well with an English audience. 'These English,' said Pepe as he left the ring, 'they don't know when something is funny.'

'And they don't recognise extraordinary musical talent when they hear it,' added Pablo.

Elena came into the ring. Clive went red. He still had a soft spot for the aerialist. She slowly climbed up the rope, her feet wrapped round, hauling herself ever upward by her strength. The music was loud. The band were playing a slow tune and Elena was gracefully moving to the music. She glided around the ring, flying high.

Then for a finale, she began to turn cartwheels in the air, over and over, the crowd counting out loudly the number of turns that she was making – twenty-nine, thirty, thirty-one – she would go on towards a hundred, when there would be an eruption of applause. Then at fifty-nine, without warning, she suddenly plummeted to the ground; her rope had snapped. There were shrieks from the audience. Elena was sprawled on the floor, limp. Pieter appeared from nowhere and ran to hold her in his arms. She was conscious, just. She was saying that her wrists felt funny, "squishy", she said. Pieter carried her behind the ring curtain. The clowns ran into the ring to distract the audience. Behind the scenes, Elena insisted that she was all right, but her hands felt painful. She passed out in Pieter's arms. He leant down and kissed her on the forehead. The circus folk surrounding her looked at one another. The couple's secret was out.

For the second time in a fortnight, an ambulance arrived at Templeton's Circus. Elena was lifted into a wheelchair and Pieter went with her to the hospital. The show went on, but Tom Parker had brought Elena's rope round the back where the circus performers had gathered. It was frayed where someone had partially cut it; when Elena had twisted it over and over, it had only been a matter of time before it snapped. The policeman who had been on guard at the circus entrance had come behind the curtain. He took one look at the frayed rope and set off to tell his superiors back at the station. Tom groaned, 'More trouble.' Was there no end to it?

The children went out into the circus zoo to get some fresh air. It hit them and winded them after the shock of seeing Elena in such discomfort. They felt sorry for her; she was so beautiful and had looked so crumpled, in pain. The show had come to the end and some of the punters were making their way into the zoo. They wanted to know how Elena was. Tom Parker addressed them; he said that she was conscious and seemed not too badly injured. It had been an accident, he said. This wasn't true and the children knew it. *But Tom must know what he was doing in lying to the crowd,* they thought. *He probably didn't want them to gossip further.*

'Could it have been Gustav?' asked Laurent. 'Could he have cut the rope?' The children looked at one another. There was seemingly no time like the present. They would confront him; see what he had to say for himself. Timmy and Olaf felt funny, uncomfortable but they were prepared to go along with the others. They made their way to his caravan but suddenly saw Gustav coming towards them, through the crowd. His face was red, tear-stained. He ran up to Timmy and Olaf and embraced them in his arms, like he was seeing them for the first time after a period of being apart. The two boys were taken aback. This wasn't like their father, for he wasn't an affectionate man – he didn't hold them, cuddle them. The gaffer appeared by Gustav's side. Tom suddenly appeared. He looked grim. Gustav was leading Timmy and Olaf back to their caravan. Tom turned to the kids.

'It's Sasha,' he said. 'She's dead.'

Twenty

A Shock!

The children didn't know what to say. *How? When? It must be a mistake!* These were the thoughts that raced through their minds. 'It wasn't anything to do with the troubles at the circus, was it?' demanded Lucy, speaking through her tears.

'No,' said Tom, 'nothing like that. She was killed in a traffic accident this afternoon. On her way back from the shops, her car collided with a lorry. She was killed outright. There was nothing anyone could have done.'

'Poor Olaf and Timmy,' said Laurent, visibly shocked.

'And poor Gustav too,' added Tom. 'Left to bring up two young boys on his own and manage the cats. It won't be easy!'

The cats, thought the children. *How would the family manage without Sasha? She had been at the centre of everything to do with the lions.*

'I'm sending Bruce over to help them get things ready for this evening's show,' indicated the ringmaster.

'This evening's show?' mumbled Annie. 'Surely they won't perform this evening.'

'Yes, they will,' said Tom. 'The show goes on. We put our makeup on and a smile; we don't let the punters see what we might be feeling on the inside. The crowds will come along at seven thirty expecting to see the lions and we won't disappoint them.'

He strode off in the direction of Gustav's caravan. The children crashed to the floor.

'Really, is that right? They will take part in the show this evening, when their mother has just died?'

'It's the circus way,' said Laurent. 'It's what we do – the show always goes on,' he added in a hollow voice.

The school kids sat there not saying a word. 'To think she risked her life every day working with lions, only to be killed in a road traffic accident,' said Clive. 'It's what Mr Baker would call *ironic*.' Those children who knew the word nodded in agreement; all were lost in their thoughts. They were each thinking of Timmy and Olaf.

'Shall we go find the boys?' asked Annie.

'Better not,' replied Pete. 'Leave them alone with their dad.' The others were secretly relieved at these words. They didn't know what they were going to say to Timmy and Olaf; they were dreading seeing them again.

Gustav! The children remembered that they had been on their way to confront him, to ask him outright if he were "the enemy within". They would have to put that thought to one side now; the man deserved their sympathy.

Timmy came running over. The children fell silent. He had been crying, they could tell. 'Listen,' he said, 'will you do you something for me?'

'Sure,' said Pete. 'Name it.'

The others nodded in agreement. Of course, they would, they would do anything.

'This business with Dad, can you put it out of your minds? If he is the one who has been behind all the trouble, we don't think he will do anything else. He's lost Mum; if it is him, he deserves to be forgiven. He's in bits.' The others weren't sure that it worked like that. Chaos and Elena were both in the local hospital, and who was to say, if it was Gustav, that he wouldn't do something else; particularly now his mind was "all over the place". 'My Auntie Isabella is coming from Solvakia. She works tigers there but will come to help us for the rest of the season. She sent a telegram as soon as she heard the news.'

The children felt as though they were playing snakes and ladders. They had landed on a snake and had slid back to square one.

'What will happen to her tigers?' asked Pete, more than a little curious.

'She will bring them with her, of course,' said Timmy. 'They will be an extra attraction in the zoo, Tom says.' The children were amazed. Timmy talked so casually about transporting tigers from another country to be with the show, as if it was all quite normal. The school children guessed it must be just that, for the circus folk were always on the move, nothing seemed to faze them.

'Is there anything we can do, mate?' asked Pete, genuinely concerned.

'You can stick around,' answered Timmy. 'It will be good to have friends about.' The school kids were pleased to hear Timmy say this. They had grown quite fond of the two lion boys that summer, and the rest of the circus children, of course.

'Sure thing,' said Pete. 'Anything. Name it!'

The crowd was beginning to gather for the seven thirty show. The children had a spot of tea with Yolanda and Natalie's parents. 'Such a shock,' said Toni. 'Sasha was such a good woman and such a wonderful mother.' The children nodded; it was true – Sasha had seemed a very good mother to her boys, and her cats. They wondered what Timmy and Olaf's Auntie Isabella would be like. Then they realised that they wouldn't know her for long because the show would be moving on. And, for the first time, the school children all thought as one: when the show moved on, they wanted to move on with it. There would be no more performances for them, no more animals; they would be going back to school, Big School – a new term of challenges and strange faces.

Pete voiced it for all of them. 'I'm going to miss all this,' he said and the other school kids nodded in agreement. They felt as though they were being left behind; it wasn't a pleasant feeling, not at all.

It was seven o'clock. The crowd had started to filter into the tent. They were buying popcorn and ice cream. The cats were to be on first. The children were pleased about that. 'Best to get it over and done with,' commented Pete.

Gustav emerged from his caravan. It seemed strange to watch him. He looked lost, as if he was missing something. And, of course, he was, Sasha. Bruce was there to help. He let the cats run down the tunnel; Gustav would be waiting at the other end. Since Chaos' accident, there was no play-acting with cuddly toys before the big beasts entered the ring. They charged down the tunnel, and the show commenced. No sooner had it begun, than the cat act was over. The lions sauntered back to their cages. No "Mother". But the show went on. It was a circus!

The following day the gaffer called a staff meeting in the big top. Tom led a prayer for Gustav and his boys. The circus folk were quiet. The Italians, French, Spanish and Irish on the show had a deep belief in God. 'Sasha is with the angels now,' whispered Toni, herself an Italian.

The gaffer ran through some business. They didn't know when the funeral would be – early next week, most likely. It would be in the morning so everyone could go and be back in time for the afternoon show. Isabella, Sasha's sister, would be arriving next week; she would be bringing four of her tigers, including a white one. This would be an added draw for the punters. 'Something to pull them in,' said the gaffer.

Then he looked serious. Tom stepped up to stand full square behind him. They were a double act, these two men. 'There is no easy way to say this,' said the gaffer. 'The other resorts further down the tour, have got cold feet. There is a lot of talk of a show that is jinxed: one that will only bring trouble to their door. If they have any excuse the towns planned for September and October will cancel our visit.'

This would mean disaster; the circus folk didn't need it spelt out. Templeton's would fold. There was a hushed silence. The performers and circus hands knew this would mean no money. Other shows all had their acts; they wouldn't need any of the performers from Templeton's – they would be approaching Christmas with no food to feed their children or animals. There was a real sense of trepidation. No-one wanted to go hungry. The crowd left the big top with grumbles and groans. There were just ten days of the Torquay stand remaining. Come Saturday week, the whole circus town would up sticks and move on. Would the trouble stop now? Or would there be more? The children didn't like to think.

On Thursday, Isabella arrived. She had driven for over two days to be with the family, as soon as she was able. She was the spitting image of Sasha, her late sister. She even sounded like her. She gave the two boys, Timmy and Olaf, a big bear hug and put her arm through Gustav's. The school kids thought it was odd. It was like Sasha had never existed. These circus folk certainly were strong. They got on with things, whatever the wind blew their way.

The tigers were beautiful and the white tiger, Josif, was a stunning animal. The school children had never seen a white tiger before; his eyes sparkled blue. He was truly magnificent. The lions seemed to know the tigers had arrived and tried to out-roar them! It was deafening, and the children could not help but laugh.

The punters came up from the town to see the white tiger. There was a hushed appreciation. Suddenly the lions looked ordinary, even the male, Deigo, with his full mane. Did the lions sense that their striped cousins were now the stars of the show? The lions lay in their cages looking lazily on, disdainful.

The weekend came and went and Tuesday arrived; it was the day of Sasha's funeral. It went as well as these things could. Gustav said something about his beloved wife and Tom spoke too. The congregation listened in silence to the two men. They sang some hymns. Timmy and Olaf sat quietly. It was hard for them. They were only young and all this seemed spookily unreal.

There were a lot of tears, but the performers were in place for the two thirty show. It was a difficult performance for them. Tom announced to the assembled audience that the show was dedicated to one of their own, the indomitable Sasha. It was hard for the circus folk. Many of them were hurting on the inside, but they had to step forward to thrill and excite.

After the seven thirty show, the circus folk were invited back to Gustav's caravan for sandwiches and a beer. Isabella helped the family to entertain their friends. They told stories of Sasha and laughed about what she had said and done – they had happy memories. They sang too. The circus folk liked to sing. They went to bed that night full of beer and stories. Their dreams were multi-coloured.

The next morning the school kids were at the ground early. There were only eleven days left of the stand. They hadn't talked about the enemy for days. It hadn't seemed right. There were other things to think about, other things to do. But now, with Sasha buried, their thoughts seemed ready to move on; not Timmy or Olaf, of course, but the others, yes, a little. The gaffer had said there were to be no more chances. If they were to see the season out, visit the towns still expecting them after Torquay, there was to be no more trouble. *Could they pull it off?*

The children liked Isabella. She had a loud laugh. Life, she said, had to go on. She was talking of mixing the lions and tigers together, to make one spectacular act for the following season. Gustav and the children would come back to Slovakia with her, she insisted. It was only right. That is where they belonged. Timmy and Olaf were unsure. They remembered their time in Slovakia. There was no pop music and fewer things to eat – certainly no chocolate, like in the English shops. Gustav just seemed ready to do whatever Isabella said. She was family and he was lost; he needed her.

By Friday evening, everything seemed to have moved on at an alarming pace. Timmy and Olaf had a new life and there was talk of a different future, and there were tigers in the zoo. One thing was the same, however. The people of Torquay turned out in numbers to see Templeton's Circus. Other towns might be thinking twice about inviting the show into their town but the people of Torquay couldn't get enough of the circus. The authorities didn't like it; they saw the show as dangerous, trouble but they didn't dare shut it down because the people of Torquay were voting with their feet.

Saturday dawned bright. It was to be a day of intrigue...

Twenty-One

Panic Stations

All the children sat back and shot lemonade into their mouths like fountains at the seafront. It was hot. The sun was blazing. It promised to be a fun day at the site. Three shows, two o'clock, five o'clock and seven thirty. They were both sold out. The children jumped up and made their way towards the tigers. As they stood there watching the sleek cats pace in their cages, they were suddenly conscious of a black taxi drawing up. It stopped outside the gaffer's caravan and out stepped a man with his arm in a sling. It was Chaos. The clown was back. The children and circus hands ran to greet him. He was a sight for sore eyes, they said. 'What did it feel like to be back?'

'Good,' he said with a grin. He wasn't wearing his wig. He seemed to be quite comfortable to appear with a completely bald head; something that he would never have done before.

Tom made his way through the crowd and slapped his hand on Chaos' back. 'Good to see you, my old friend,' he exclaimed. There was a buzz, an excitement for the circus folk were pleased to see one of their own return. This so called "enemy" wouldn't beat them; they were made of sterner stuff!

Chaos disappeared into the gaffer's caravan with Tom. They would have a lot to talk about. So much happened: Sasha's death; Bella's escape; Elena's fall – her romance with Pieter…

'I wonder when he will be back in the show?' questioned Pete.

'Next week,' said Laurent. 'You see.'

'But his arm, it's in a sling,' said Annie.

'So?' said Timmy. 'That won't stop him. He has sawdust in his veins. He won't be able to hear the sound of the audience and stay out of the big top.' The school kids looked at one another. The man was injured. How could he perform, for heaven's sake? Still, the gaffer would be pleased; it would mean he could let Pepe and Pablo go!

Isabella walked by. She called to her tigers. They muzzled up against the bars of their cages. She ruffled their fur. Josif let out a low groan. He really was an impressive creature.

The children headed into the big top where the last of the performers were finishing their practice. Pieter was there. He looked miserable. *He will be missing Elena,* thought the children. The news on Elena had been bad, but not disastrous. She had broken both wrists; she was black and blue, swollen, but she would recover. However, the circus folk couldn't be sure that she would ever perform in the air again. What would she do? If she couldn't be in the show, what was there for her; she had been performing in the circus since the age of eight and she knew nothing else.

The morning wore on. The children ate their lunch in the shade of a tree. George the giraffe was munching upon the leaves of a branch that someone had chopped down for him. The campsite was still. On the breeze, came the chants of the cranks at the front gate: 'What do we want? Animals out! When do we want it? Now, now, now.' The antis had been incensed that the show now had tigers, especially a white one – it was a disgrace, they argued! They were calling on the people of Torquay to turn away. A few listened, most ignored them.

Two o'clock came and the band struck up its opening fanfare. The crowd got behind the performers, willing them on. In Elena's absence, the fliers now had two turns. The crowd marvelled at their death defying grace. During the interval, the school kids were invited to help sell ice cream and popcorn; they felt like they really belonged.

The second half opened with George, followed by the stallions. Chaos sat in the front row, soaking up the atmosphere; if ever there was a man pleased to be back, it was him. He beamed throughout the whole performance; the children could sense that he was thinking, *Next week, this will be me*. The lions were last. Isabella was now helping Gustav instead of Bruce. She was an old hand at showing cats. The lions responded to her strong confident voice and Gustav seemed content to have her standing outside the cage door, keeping an ever-watchful eye on the five lions.

After the show, around a hundred or so punters filled the zoo. There was no doubt that the tigers were the star draw. Isabella beamed. The children moved off and flopped down outside Toni and Orlando's caravan. Tom was doing the rounds, telling the circus folk that the gaffer had yet again sent out for dinner for all of them, chicken, chips and beer! The performers and hands came out to sprawl in front of their wagons. One week left of a six-week stand. And, what a stand it had been! They laid back in the late afternoon sunshine, laughing and joking. Despite someone's best efforts, the circus had been a success. Now, fingers crossed, they would see out the remaining week and then head on to the autumn run of resorts – Plymouth, Bournemouth, Southampton, Southsea, Brighton and Eastbourne – nine weeks before the end of what had been a very long season.

As they lay in the warmth, the circus children began to talk of their plans for the winter season. Timmy and Olaf were off to Slovakia – to train the lions and tigers to work together in a mixed act of nine big cats. Natalie and Yolanda were going to the Cirque d'Hiver in Paris where their parents would perform till March. Laurent was to stay with Templeton's Circus in their winter quarters, and tour with them next year. Natalie and Yolanda would then move on to a Spanish Circus, Gran Circo Mundial, for the 1975 season. Pete knew it because Natalie had already told him. They were booked to come back to Templeton's in 1976. But by then, they would be thirteen. *Natalie would have forgotten all about him*, he thought, *should she ever return to Torquay.*

As they sat in the balmy evening, they chatted and laughed. Tom came round with more drinks: cans of Coke for the children, something stronger for the grown-ups. Gustav and Isabella came to sit with them. Gustav seemed sad enough but Isabella seemed determined to cheer him up; it was, she said, what her sister would have wanted. Timmy and Olaf looked at their father. They loved him. They probably hadn't realised just how much until they had lost their mother. He was now all they had – they didn't count Isabella, well not just yet, not fully.

They were suddenly all hit by a wall of intense heat. Like a gust from a furnace. It prickled their skin and made them scratch as if they were sore. They didn't like to breathe, for fear of burning their mouths and nostrils. What was happening? What was it? They suddenly heard loud pitch squealing from the elephants. Fire! The elephant stable was ablaze. They could see flames dancing high into the sky, billowing black smoke. Manu ran to the tent; outside stood two fire extinguishers. He tried one; it had been tampered with. He tried the next; it too had been bodged. Seeing the elephant trainer's desperate predicament, Gustav was up in seconds, dashing to the water tap. 'Quick,' he screamed, 'buckets!' The hands ran to the mess tent and emerged holding pails. 'C'mon,' shouted Gustav, taking control. 'Buckets to me, then get in a line.'

The circus folk clambered over one another to pick up a bucket and deposited them with Gustav, who started to fill them. The hands passed the pails brimming with water down the line, propelling them towards the tent, where Isabella stood bravely at the end of the line, throwing each one in turn at the fire. The children picked up the empty buckets and ran them back to Gustav who refilled them so they could be passed along the line again. Again and again, they went. Meanwhile, Manu and Bruce had entered the tent seemingly without a thought for their personal safety. Seconds later, three elephants stampeded into the safety of the zoo, charging forward with trunks extended, trumpeting for all they were worth. And then the fire was out, smouldering and hissing, but out. The danger had passed. The circus folk began to cheer and whoop. Manu, Bruce and Gustav were each holding onto an elephant, talking them down, calming them. Isabella fell to the floor, coughing and spluttering, holding her sides, short of breath – her chest painful to the touch. The zoo sounded like the African jungle; all the animals were sounding off – the cats were roaring, clawing at their cages, fighting. Gustav shouted to get water on them to quieten them down, split them up; it worked. The stable hands each ran to their charges, spoke to them, soothed them.

The circus folk sat back down on the grass. They were exhausted, spent. What a to-do! Tom appeared and quietly asked people to gather in the big top. The gaffer would speak to them. It was hot in the tent and the performers and hands were tired from their exertions. They collapsed, dirty and hot, into the seating and the gaffer came forward into the ring, the microphone in his hand. 'Well done, everyone,' he said. There was some applause. 'That could have been very nasty,' he continued. 'Our elephants are priceless – my thanks to Gustav who organised us so well.' There were loud cheers and cries of *For he's a jolly good fellow*. The children looked down at the ground. Only last week they had suspected Gustav. Tom had thought too that he could be the one who was behind all the trouble. How silly the children felt now.

Gustav was nothing short of a hero. Without him, goodness knows what would have happened. The gaffer tried to quieten the crowd down but they were having none of it. They had something to cheer about and they were going to make themselves heard. 'Listen,' said the gaffer, again appealing for quiet. 'We have to keep what happened here today to ourselves. We cannot afford for the news to get out that there was again trouble at Templeton's Circus. One whiff of this to the authorities and we will be blocked from going to any more sites this season. This fire never happened. It is our secret. Do I have your word on that?'

There were shouts of 'Yes,' and 'Sure thing, Boss.'

'Good,' said the gaffer. 'Now let's clear up the mess and then spend a quiet evening in front of our caravans. Tomorrow is Sunday. There is just one more week of our stay here in Torquay and then we move on.'

The circus folk filed out of the tent and set to the dirty job of clearing up the mess from the fire. The elephants had been given a makeshift home on the other side of the zoo; they were reluctant to go anywhere near their old home. Manu said he would be spending the night camped out with them and, much to the trainer's surprise, Bruce said he would be joining them. The elephants seemed content enough, their adventure over.

The school kids sat down with their circus friends at the end of what had been another eventful day. Gustav, whom they had suspected, and Bruce, had both shown themselves to be friends of the circus. What a pickle this was! Just when you thought you had solved the mystery, events proved you wrong. Where would it all end? The children thought it lucky that the policeman assigned to the gate had made for home after the end of the last show of the day; if he hadn't, the news of the fire would have spread and Templeton's Circus would have had no towns to visit after the Torquay season had come to an end.

The school kids said their goodbyes and started the long walk home. They seemed to have reached a dead end. They had no suspects left. What were they to do next?

Twenty-Two

A Familiar Face

The children were determined to spend as much of their time as possible at the circus in the last week of the Torquay stay. They gathered early on Sunday morning in the big top. Isabella was practising her tigers. The children sat watching, entranced. At the end of the act, Josif, the white tiger, sat up on a shiny, silver ball which turned round slowly under a spotlight. It was breathtaking; only Pete and Natalie thought it looked rather sad, tawdry. The children began to chat about their next move. With only a week left, they wondered if they would ever identify "the enemy within". Had they finished disrupting the show, whoever they were? Or were there more twists and turns to come in this last six days? The gaffer had spelt out to people just how important it was that there was no more trouble. Templeton's Circus could afford no further scandal.

The children listed the suspects they had discounted: Demetrius, Bruce, Chaos, Pieter, Elena and Gustav. They felt a little ashamed to have thought the worst of these people. It felt uncomfortable. Still, they had meant no harm. They were just trying to solve the mystery.

'Well, where do we go next?' asked Pete. No-one spoke because it was difficult to see where they should go next.

'Shall we talk to Tom?' suggested Natalie.

'None of his suspects are in the frame,' said Pete. 'Pieter wouldn't have injured Elena; Bruce and Gustav wouldn't have saved the elephants from the fire.'

It was true. They were stumped. 'We need an adult to talk it through with,' said Yolanda. 'We might be missing something.' The children were all in agreement, but who?

'I know,' said Pete, suddenly excited. 'How 'bout Mr Baker?' The school children broke into a collective smile. Good old Mr Baker. They were very fond of him. But they didn't have the faintest idea where he lived. How could they find out? 'We could look in the telephone book,' suggested Pete. 'How many Mr Bakers can there be?'

There were five: an E Baker, two S Bakers, a W Baker and a T E Baker. The addresses were all shown but the children were despondent. They couldn't visit them all and no-one felt like phoning each one; it would cost money and besides it would be easier to speak to someone face to face. They thought round the problem. 'What does he look like?' said Natalie. 'A Stephen, a William? I think he looks like a William,' she said.

The others thought. Look there are two living quite close to one another and one has the initial W. Why don't we visit those? They're within walking distance. If it's not one, it might be the other. It seemed like a plan; the best one that they could think of, at any rate. They set off, all nine of them. Pete and Lucy knew the way, the others followed. They reached the first address after twenty minutes or so. 'Who will go up and knock on the door?' asked Pete. 'We can't all go marching up – we'll look silly if it isn't him.'

To decide, they threw coins to see who could get closest to a wall. Lucy and Clive were the furthest away. They would knock. The two children nervously walked up the path. They rang the doorbell. A little old lady came to the door. A cat played around at her feet. 'We're looking for Mr Baker, our school teacher,' said Lucy.

'Doesn't live here, sweetie,' said the woman, 'just me and Jasper,' she pointed to the cat.

'Sorry to trouble you,' said Clive. The children walked back down the path, relieved it had only been a little old lady; they had been worried the person opening the door to them might be rude – not everyone wanted strangers turning up on their doorstep. 'No good,' said Clive.

Pete knew where the next address was. It was just a couple of streets away. We have a one in four chance of it being Mr Baker said Annie knowledgeably for she had recently done probability; so had the other school kids, but they still weren't sure she was right. They approached the house, number thirty-one. Laurent and Pete volunteered to go up to the door. They knocked as there was no bell.

Mr Baker opened the door. Success.

The two boys grinned. Mr Baker was clearly a little taken aback to see the children. 'Who is it?' floated a voice from inside the house.

Mr Baker scratched his head. 'Some kids from school,' he replied.

'Who?' came the voice, sounding surprised. A woman appeared. She looked nice enough. The two adults were amazed to see the remaining seven kids come slowly up the path.

'Wow,' said Mr Baker. 'What can I do for you kids?'

They all spoke at once. He heard – 'circus… enemy… Chaos… injury… gaffer.'

'Whooa,' he said. He turned to the woman. 'They had better come in.' She nodded, laughing.

'Into the garden,' he said. 'They'll be room for all of you there.' They went through the hallways and then into the kitchen. There was a door which Mr Baker opened, and the children proceeded out into the garden. They squatted on the grass. The woman, who was introduced to them as Mrs Baker, the teacher's wife, appeared with a jug of lemonade and biscuits. 'Right,' said Mr Baker. 'From the beginning, one at a time please.'

They put their hands up; they were in school mode now. He chose Pete, who started the tale. The children relayed how they had followed first Chaos, then Pieter and Elena. Mr Baker laughed when he heard about the wig shop; his wife sighed when she heard about Pieter and Elena kissing outside the restaurant. 'How romantic,' she said and the girls nodded.

The Bakers had read of Chaos being attacked in the newspaper. How was he? they asked. The children explained that he seemed friendlier since the accident. 'Ironic,' said Mr Baker, his favourite word; the children noted it and smiled. The two grown-ups had seen the elephants swim at the sea on the news. The news of the circus' troubles had made it into the Bakers' home that summer but they hadn't imagined for a second that some of the school kids would be involved.

'You've had six suspects,' said Mrs Baker. 'Who else is there left to suspect?' The children listed the performers at the show who they knew: the three remaining fliers, Toni and Orlando (Natalie and Yolanda blushed at their parents' mention); then there were some ring boys, but they had all been with the circus for years, said Laurent.

'You don't really have anything to go on, do you?' noted Mr Baker. The children sighed. He was right. Did he have any advice for them? He was a teacher. Teachers were good at that. 'Well,' he said, 'someone has been pretty determined to ruin the show, haven't they? They have been prepared to cause disruption and even injury. Chaos and Elena could have been killed; it doesn't bear thinking about!'

The children gulped their lemonade. 'Today is Sunday,' he went on. 'The show finishes its stand on Saturday. Six days remaining. If I were the enemy, I would be planning my next step very carefully. If I was determined to get the show shut down this summer, I have only a few days remaining to pull it off. My next step could be my last chance.' The children looked at one another. Mr Baker was right. Who knows what the enemy would have planned but, like as not, there would be something. And, it would be big.

'We had better get back to the show,' said Laurent. They thanked Mr and Mrs Baker for the lemonade and biscuits and made their way through the house to the door.

'You kids, be careful,' urged Mr Baker. 'This all sounds pretty dangerous to me.'

Mr Baker closed the door after the children. He looked at his wife. 'You have no choice,' she murmured, 'they're kids at the end of the day.' He nodded. He picked up the phone that stood in the doorway and thumbed through the phone directory. Slowly, he dialled the number for the local police station.

Back at the camp, there was a disturbance outside the ground. The cranks were there, led by the Dave fellow and were making a lot of noise. Isabella was there. She was shouting at Dave, but he wasn't listening to Isabella. He was shouting at her and she wasn't listening to him. He had a large poster of a white tiger behind bars; someone had drawn a clown's hat on the animal. Isabella was red, getting redder. Gustav was there. He was pulling Isabella back. Suddenly, she snatched the poster off a protester and threw it into the ditch. She was spitting like a Catherine wheel. Dave shoved her. She toppled backwards and hit her head on the ground. She was conscious, but seemingly dazed. Tom sat her up; a bump had come up on her head, like an egg. Tom was talking to her all the while, keeping her from drifting off. Gustav was furious but before he could punch this Dave character, the sentry policeman, who had been watching from afar, stepped in. 'None of that, sir,' he ordered. 'Now everyone calm down.'

He looked at Isabella sitting on the floor. He turned to Dave. 'I am arresting you, sir.'

'What?' said Dave. 'You must be joking. All I did was give her a little push.'

'Yes, sir, you did, and as a consequence the lady fell and is hurt. You must accompany me to the station.' And stepping back, he motioned to the animal rights' protester to step forward down the road. He radioed for a police car to come and collect them. The circus folk who were gathered round began to cheer.

'No, no, no,' said the policeman. 'If the lady wasn't incapacitated, I'd arrest her for damage to property,' and quickly added, seeing the puzzled looks of the circus folk, 'that poster is ruined!' The children wanted to laugh but the sight of a stern policeman and an injured Isabella made them think better of it. Isabella was now on her feet and was being helped back into the circus ground, one arm round Tom, the other, Gustav. She was moving gingerly. The children followed on afterwards. Isabella was talking ten to the dozen. She wasn't making much sense.

'Zes cranks,' she exclaimed. 'In Slovakia, we would be shutting them all up and throwing away the lock.' The children thought she probably meant to say key, but they didn't like to correct her. Gustav helped her up the steps into his caravan. The gaffer appeared. He wanted a word with Gustav. He wasn't happy, the children could tell. He was speaking quietly to the lion tamer. The children couldn't hear what he was saying, but they could guess he was warning Gustav that he had better get Isabella under control, or she would be on the first boat back to Slovakia! What a day. First they had met with success, finding Mr Baker, only to find poor Isabella take a knock to the head. Gustav appeared. He jogged down the steps and headed in the direction of Toni's caravan.

'Maybe he wants Mum's advice,' said Natalie. 'She used to be a nurse before she met Dad and came into the circus.' The children looked up, their interest aroused. They hadn't known that Toni had not been born into the circus. She was what circus folk called a "Yosser", someone who had not been born into the show. The children were all thinking the same thing, all but Natalie and Yolanda.

The two girls looked up. 'Why are you all staring at us?' asked Natalie. Then the penny dropped. 'You can't think it's our mum,' she burst out, her eyes wide like saucers.

'That's exactly how Timmy and I felt when you suspected our dad,' replied Olaf. The school children looked awkward. This accusing of family members was uncomfortable business; they didn't want to offend Natalie and Yolanda, that was the last thing that they wanted, especially Pete; Natalie was his girlfriend, after all.

'It's just a thought,' said Lucy. 'Maybe someone who isn't circus through and through, might be more likely to try to ruin one.'

'But for what reason?' came back Natalie, angrily. The children fell silent. They didn't have a reason as to why Toni might have done these terrible things, but just for now, her face might fit; *and besides*, they thought, *we have no-one else to suspect.*

Twenty-Three

Josif

Monday morning found the school kids at the site early. Isabella and Gustav were talking to their cats. Gustav had his arm around Isabella's waist. Did this mean they were an item? It looked for all the world like Gustav had replaced his late wife with her sister. The school kids were taken aback. Circus life: everything moved so quickly.

As they stood watching the tigers with the happy couple, a white car trundled slowly over the ground. It was a big car, a Rolls Royce said Pete, who knew about such things. The car drew to a halt and a driver got out. He looked fairly ordinary looking, too ordinary to be driving such a posh car. He skipped to the back passenger seat and opened it. The children realised he must be the chauffeur. *Who was this who had come to visit Templeton's?* A fat man in a ten-gallon hat got out. He was smoking a large cigar.

'Hey, kids,' he shouted. 'Which is Tom Parker's caravan?' Laurent nodded towards Tom's caravan. The man waddled to the steps and having climbed them, knocked on Tom's door. Tom opened it and the man went in, clearly exhausted from the effort, for he was sweating, wiping his forehead with a giant red hankie.

'Who is it?' wondered Lucy.

Gustav knew. 'It's Billy Bright,' he said. *Billy Bright, the owner of Bright's Circus. What was he doing here?* Tom's caravan door opened and the two men came down the steps. They made their way to the gaffer's caravan and entered. A few of the circus folk came up and stood around the caravan. They were quickly joined by others, and then, more. There was soon quite a crowd. Word had got round that Billy Bright was in the camp.

Suddenly there were raised voices from inside. The children could hear Tom's voice. Then the door opened. Tom could be heard, telling the gaffer to calm down. Billy Bright came flying down the steps and hurried to his car: a fat man, he looked like he might stumble – like a hippo with carrots in his sights. Tom was having to hold the gaffer back. 'And, don't come back in a hurry,' the circus boss was shouting, 'unless you intend to buy a ticket!'

Billy Bright, back in the safety of his car wound down the window and yelled to the gaffer, 'You'll regret not selling, soon you won't be able to give your show away.' With that, he motioned to the driver to put his foot down, and the white Rolls Royce left the ground, more quickly than it had arrived.

The gathered circus folk began to mumble and grumble. What was going on? The gaffer came to the top of the steps: 'Staff meeting,' he barked and strode in the direction of the big top. The crowd chased after him, like goslings following their mother. Tom brought up the rear. The children sat at the back; they had learnt to keep out of the way when there looked like trouble between the grown-ups. 'Listen,' said the gaffer, taking to the microphone. 'You all saw him. That was that blighter Billy Bright. He's just insulted me. He offered me £10,000 for my show, lock stock and barrel.'

The crowd were silent. They didn't want the gaffer to sell; they knew there might be jobs for some of them with Billy Bright but others would be out of work. He already had lions of his own and elephants and fliers! The crowd began to applaud the gaffer. All except Tom, who stepped up to speak. 'That's all well and good,' he said, taking the microphone, 'but we can't afford any more mishaps.' Isabella went red and her gaze hit the floor; she was remembering her altercation with Dodgy Dave. 'We must be on our guard,' said Tom. The gaffer nodded. 'If the cranks try and wind you up, ignore them,' pleaded Tom. 'Everyone keep your head down and get on with your work.' The crowd started to break up, making their way back to their caravans with plenty of food for thought.

'Let's head for the beach,' suggested Laurent. 'This is our last free day in Torquay, we should make the most of it.'

'Good idea,' agreed Pete, and slipped his hand into Natalie's. Both she and Yolanda had been quiet; they didn't like to think that suspicion had fallen upon their mother. Still no-one had mentioned it again.

She smiled. 'Yes,' she said. 'Let's go for a swim.'

It was hot and the forecast was for a week that would get hotter and hotter. The children ran to get their things, plus some costumes for the circus kids. The beach was packed, full of pink holidaymakers having fun. The children were reminded of the day they had brought the elephants to paddle; that had been such fun. The children enjoyed a lazy afternoon. They swam, sunbathed, swam, sunbathed, and swam some more. Natalie kissed Pete in full sight of the other kids. Laurent looked a little annoyed but the others whooped. They had all become firm friends over the past six weeks; it seemed like they had known one another all their lives.

When they got back to the camp, Isabella and Gustav, helped by Bruce, were erecting Isabella's ring cage in the middle of the zoo. 'What are you up to, Dad?' asked Timmy, intrigued.

'Isabella's idea,' he laughed. 'We have a spare ring cage, Isabella thought it would be good to let the cats take turns to use it as an exercise area – get them out of the van – it's so hot.'

The children thought this a great idea, especially Pete and Natalie. 'It's a great idea, give the cats somewhere to play,' said Pete. 'All circuses should do this, all the time.'

Timmy wasn't so sure. Their cats slept most of the day, what did they need an exercise area for?

Natalie thought he was missing the point. 'Even if they only play for a short while, that's a good thing, surely,' she insisted.

Josif was the first cat down into the exercise cage; he went bounding to the side and reached up against the cage bars, leaning forward on tiptoes full stretch, his belly exposed.

'See,' said Pete, 'he's lovin' it.'

Timmy wasn't sure. He would be a cat man when he was older: putting up an exercise cage would mean effort and money – you'd have to buy a second cage and then spend time putting it up; he didn't think it was practical at all.

'How 'bout the ladies?' asked Lucy. 'They must be hot inside.' Could they do something for them?

'Hot yes,' said Laurent, 'but elephants need the shade.'

Lucy wasn't satisfied with the answer. 'But you could give them an exercise pen *with* some shade instead of being chained in a tent.'

The circus kids frowned, all except Natalie. They didn't like where this conversation was going. 'We know how to take care of our animals,' said Timmy, firmly. 'We don't need outsiders to tell us how to improve things.' The school kids were deflated. They hadn't meant to upset their circus friends. They didn't like being called *outsiders*.

'Come on,' said Natalie. 'Let's not fall out.'

'No,' pleaded Pete. 'Let's not.'

'Why don't we ask the gaffer for some sandwiches for tea, with some pop?' suggested Laurent.

'Dare we?' asked Timmy. 'The gaffer didn't look too pleased this morning, he might not have calmed down.'

'I'll ask,' offered Laurent. 'I'm the oldest.'

He bombed up the gaffer's stairs. He stood talking to him. The gaffer's face broke into a broad smile, he was nodding. Laurent swaggered back to where his friends were sitting on the grass. 'Beef sandwich tea for everyone, with pop for us and beer for the grown-ups,' he declared triumphantly. The gaffer gave the word and sandwiches were rustled up by the ladies who ran the snack wagon; they always kept supplies of cold beef, just in case the gaffer felt generous. All the circus folk came out on to the grass in front of their caravans and threw down blankets. Some had radios that they played and some began to dance. They were in good spirits.

After they had eaten their tea someone gave a shout, 'Let's form the human pyramid.' The school kids didn't know what was meant by this.

'Sit back and watch,' said Laurent. 'Let's see if we can get to four storeys high, we made it last time!' The circus kids scrambled to their feet and ran to the middle ground. Pieter took control. First some of the larger men knelt down in a line. Onto their backs climbed the taller men. They put their arms around one another's backs and drew close. Then, onto their shoulders climbed the smaller women, and finally onto their shoulders climbed up the children, who stood aloft, waving their hands in the air, shouting.

'Quick,' shouted Toni, 'a photo.' Orlando ran forward with his camera and beckoned the school kids to stand in front of the motley crew. Snap taken, at a shout from Pieter, the pyramid fell forward. The school children gasped. Surely someone would end up with broken bones. But these were circus folk. They all knew how to fall; they rolled into balls and jumped into the air, shouting and screaming in laughter.

The circus children came running over to their school friends. They collapsed down onto the floor, laughing. 'It's our party piece,' said Laurent, with a grin.

'Some party piece,' said Pete. 'All my mum and dad do is play the spoons.' The children laughed at the thought of Pete's parents with a pair of spoons in their hands, trying to eke out a tune by banging them together on their legs.

'Sorry about earlier,' said Pete.

'Yeh, sorry,' chorused the other school kids.

'No problem,' said Laurent. 'It's just that we get a bit fed up with people telling us how to care for our animals. We love them.'

'We know,' acknowledged Pete. 'We just meant it would be nice for the animals to have exercise areas.'

Natalie could see the argument starting again. 'Are you looking forward to going back to school?' she asked, deftly changing the subject.

'What do you think?' replied Lucy, and the children burst out laughing.

'I'm worried,' admitted Clive, 'that I might get bullied. Everyone pokes fun at the fat kid. My mum says we're going from being big fish in a little pond, to small fish in a big pond.' The others sat and thought it through.

'Yes, I guess you are going to be small fish,' confessed Laurent.

'And how 'bout you?' asked Lucy. 'Are you looking forward to your next school?'

'Never do we look forward to that,' said Laurent. 'Though this last time was different: we made friends — you!' The school kids smiled.

They lay back in the late afternoon sun. They closed their eyes and pointed their heads toward the sky. With their eyes closed, they became more conscious of the sounds around them: a lion's roar, or was it a tiger's (Timmy and Olaf knew, of course); the circus folk laughing and joking; the sound of the circus generator, switched on to illuminate the front of the show, where punters stood at the booking office, buying their seats for the last week of the stand. Happy days!

Suddenly the sounds were punctuated by a large piercing scream. The children bolted upright. *What now?* Gustav shot past them and they instinctively got up to follow him. He ran to Isabella who was stood by the exercise cage that they had erected earlier that afternoon. The children pushed past the crowd who had gathered around the bars, fighting their way forward so that they could see: there lying in the middle of the cage, was Josif. He was dead; the children could see that straight away. His body lay lifeless, his blue tongue hanging towards the ground. By him lay some half eaten meat. 'My Josif,' screamed Isabella, 'he's been poisoned.' The children looked from Gustav to Isabella to Timmy to Olaf. How much more could one family take?

Tom came running up. The gaffer pushed his way through the crowd. He surveyed the scene. He clocked the dead tiger. 'We sort this ourselves,' he said. 'No police, nobody, but us.'

Twenty-Four

A Storm

Tuesday was hotter than Monday. When the gaffer had said, "We'll sort this," what he had meant was, we'll get rid of the tiger, we won't tell anyone about it. He hadn't meant, we'll find the culprit. How could he have? He didn't have the faintest idea who was behind the campaign to derail his circus. No-one did – certainly not the children. Their only remaining suspect, Toni, had been sitting with them on the grass all afternoon. She hadn't had the opportunity to poison Josif. Isabella was dreadfully upset. She had prized the white cat; it had been her pride and joy. The children thought she seemed more upset about the loss of the tiger than her sister. But then they reproached themselves for the thought – they were being mean. She had loved both her sister and Josif; it wasn't right to compare them.

The crowds flocked to the shows on Tuesday and Wednesday. The children were at each performance and stood together in the zoo afterwards. They remembered what Tom had said: "No more mishaps". The gaffer had made it clear that they couldn't afford any. Any more scandal and the remaining towns on the tour would tumble like dominoes – each would say no to the circus' planned visit. There would be no money from ticket sales; no food on the table; no Christmas treats at the end of what had already been a long season.

But nothing happened. Before they knew it, it was Thursday morning.

'Elena,' exclaimed Lucy when the children met up, 'let's ask Pieter how she is.' They headed for Pieter's caravan. He was just emerging from his door. The children stopped in their tracks, for he was wearing a suit and tie. They weren't used to seeing circus folk look like that. He was holding on tightly to a bunch of flowers.

'How is Elena, Pieter?' asked Annie. The acrobat looked excited, if a little nervous.

'I am just on my way to see her,' he replied and then proudly added, 'to ask her to be my wife.' With this he produced a tiny box and, opening it, showed the children a ring that sparkled.

'Ohhh,' said the girls in unison. Now, it was their turn to look excited.

'Wish me luck,' he cried and hurried out towards the gate.

The children wandered over to Toni and Orlando's caravan. Toni was there, sitting on the steps, reading a magazine. She looked up when she heard the children and smiled. 'What's your news?' she asked. They told her about Pieter. 'Really?' she said, jumping up, with excitement. 'But we must throw a party for him when he returns

When Pieter returned early in the evening, he was beaming. Elena had said, "Yes". The girls were overjoyed. Clive didn't get it, or Timmy. What was all the fuss about? The circus folk gathered round the acrobat and there was a lot of backslapping. The beer was broken out and before long the performers and ring hands were singing. This lasted long into the evening. They finished with a rousing rendition of "I'm getting married in the morning, ding dong the bells are gonna chime".

That week, the people had come, the performers had shone. By the end of the week, the circus folk were beginning to relax. It was nearly Saturday and they were almost there – the day that would mark the end of the Torquay summer season. The weather grew hotter still – clammy, airless. The children spent Friday afternoon lazing on the verge outside the cats' makeshift exercise cage. It was fun to watch them gambol on the grass. Gustav had introduced a large tyre into the cage and the cats did not tire of pulling it about in the evening sunshine; jumping on it, seizing the rubber in their jaws.

Was that it? Had the enemy given up? Thrown the towel in, leaving Templeton's show to move freely on to the autumn leg of their tour?

'If I were the enemy,' said Laurent, 'I would be planning one last effort like Mr Baker said. I wouldn't have done so much, only to give up!'

Pete stirred on the grass, making himself more comfortable. 'What would you be planning?' he asked, his eyes shut to the sun.

'Something big,' replied Laurent.

'When would you do it?' asked Natalie.

'Tomorrow night,' said Laurent, 'Saturday night, the last night of the stand. Go out with a bang. Boom!'

The children sat up. 'Of course,' said Annie. 'That's why he hasn't done anything this week; he's waiting till the last night. He'll get maximum impact. The newspaper would love the story: "Disaster at the big top on its final night".'

'Yes,' said Pete, 'I can see the headlines now. *They were almost there, had nearly made it, but then tragedy struck…*'

'Wait, I've had a brilliant idea,' blurted out Annie. She was so excited she could barely get her words out in any sensible order. She spoke quickly, ever so quickly: 'Saturday night,' she said, 'us, you, a sleepover; we could stay late, till the early hours, keep watch.' The children got the gist of what she was trying to say. *A sleepover.* It was a great idea.

'But where would we sleep?' demanded Pete. 'We wouldn't all fit in your caravans.'

'Outside, of course. We often sleep outside. Why, I've been out all this week, it's been so hot,' shot Laurent with a sparkle in his eye.

The children were excited. It was a brilliant way to end their time together and most importantly they might finally catch the enemy. The school kids hurried home to beg their parents. All said yes, apart from Lucy's mum and dad, who thought she had been spending far too much time already at that "jinxed show". She was desperately disappointed but the circus children invited her for breakfast on Sunday morning. It was something, a chance to say goodbye properly. However, it didn't take away the upset she felt to be missing out.

Saturday dawned close and humid. The children spent the day looking forward to the evening. They were to come to the site at six thirty with their sleeping bags, in time to soak up the atmosphere behind the red curtains. They were there at six o'clock; they just couldn't wait any longer. Toni had spoken to the gaffer, who had given permission for the kids to stay over; they had become a familiar sight during the show's stay and the circus folk liked them.

The final show was scheduled for seven thirty. It was traditional at the end of a long run for the performers to play practical jokes on one another. Somebody (Toni) had hidden Chaos' wig; someone (Pieter) had put ice cubes into a flier's top; someone else (Chaos) had swapped a carrot for Tom's microphone. All these tricks put the performer who was the butt of the joke at a disadvantage: Chaos had to go on bald (he laughed about it where once he would have been furious); Delores got very cold "up top", even when she had pulled the ice cubes out, and Tom had frantically searched for the microphone, which he eventually found hidden in his hat.

The audience was packed. They loved the show. The performers were relaxed and the animals seemed to sense that they would be on the move again tomorrow; already their lorries were being loaded with their props at the end of the performance. The animals knew what that meant: they were off! The crowd gave the show a standing ovation. The performers came behind the curtain after the show, whooping and punching the air. The Torquay season, despite all the mishaps, had pulled the crowds in. They would be off tomorrow to a different town. They had kept going. Despite the best efforts of "someone" to ensure that the tour stopped right here, right now, in Torquay – finished its run early – folded, but despite everything, they were ready for the move.

The children had stayed alert during the show, as had the gaffer, who was at the curtains watching the show during the whole performance, something he never did. Did he sense too that this might be the night that the enemy would strike? One last attempt to ruin Templeton's?

The children walked out into the night and they were met by a surprising sight. It was raining. For the first time in weeks they could feel the pitter-patter of drops falling on their faces. They went back and stood on the underside of the tent, looking out. Performers ran for their caravans. Then it started to really pour down. It was still hot, close, and the circus folk were shouting that it looked like thunder. 'We'll have to sleep in the elephant tent,' said Laurent. 'We'll need cover.'

Sleeping in an elephant tent – how unexpected. They ran for the entrance. Manu was there and Bruce. 'What are you kids doing?' asked the trainer, surprised to see them. They explained that the gaffer had said they could sleep over. He shrugged his shoulders. 'Don't you keep my ladies awake with your laughter and chat,' he said, with a grimace. 'They need their beauty sleep,' he added, with a sudden grin. Two of the elephants were lying on their sides, their eyes open, their ears flapping to keep themselves cool. The third elephant stood swaying. 'She's on guard,' said Manu. 'They will take it in turns.'

The children exchanged glances. Of course, that is what they would have to do: take it in turns to stay awake, on watch in the zoo and big top, looking for danger. Perhaps the enemy meant to set fire to the circus tent? Perhaps he meant to let a tiger loose? Do something that would hit the front pages of the newspaper and be the lead story on the local news. Something that would get the remaining towns on the tour to shut up shop – refuse entry to Templeton's show.

Who amongst them would take the first watch?

Manu and Bruce had gone. The children discussed their plans quietly, so as not to disturb the three listening elephants. Laurent and Clive would go to the big top, stay till two o'clock, when Annie and Pete would take over. Natalie and Timmy would sit out in the zoo, or rather lie in their sleeping bags, underneath Toni and Orlando's caravan. They would, again, stay till two, when Olaf and Yolanda would relieve them from duty. They set the alarms on their LED digital watches and either bedded down in the elephant tent or went outside to take up their position.

The rain was getting harder. The circus folk had all gone to bed. Lights were off in each caravan. The children crept to their places. The big top was eerie, with no lights except the beam from Laurent and Clive's torch. Underneath Toni and Orlando's caravan, Natalie and Timmy lay on their tummies, keeping a watch out into the darkness. By midnight, all the children, on watch or not, were fast asleep. At two, their alarms sounded quietly, but loud enough to wake them. They struggled to their feet and, without a sound, exchanged places. 'Nothing to report,' whispered Natalie to Olaf and Yolanda.

'Nothing doing,' hissed Laurent to Annie and Pete.

Now wide awake, the new sentries came on duty. There was a flash of lightning. Olaf counted. *One, two, three, four.* Then there was a clap of thunder. 'The storm is four miles away,' he breathed. It was something that Sasha had taught him and for the first time that particular day, he thought of his mother. He missed her. Isabella was a comfort but she wasn't Mum. Another flash of lightning. *One, two, three.* A louder roll of thunder.

'It's getting closer,' Laurent whispered to Yolanda. The animals were stirring. The sides of the beast wagons were up but the children sensed that the cats were awake, pacing behind them.

'Cats don't like storms,' said Olaf.

Yolanda nodded.

A third flash of lightning. *One, two,* counted Olaf. Crash, came the thunder, much louder now. It would be overhead shortly. The cats would go mental. The rain became harder; it bounced off the wagons' roofs. Then there came a fourth flash, stronger than all the others. It lit up the zoo and for a brief second the two children caught sight of a man by George the giraffe's enclosure. There was an almighty bang, as the storm reached directly overhead. The two children scrambled up. They stepped out into the rain. It ran down their faces and poured off the end of their chins. Another flash of lightning, and there was the shadowy figure again. In the light, the children could see that he had pulled open the gate and was marshalling George through the gap, clapping his hands, herding the giraffe out into the open zoo.

'Quick,' said Yolanda, 'after him.' The children began to run. Olaf, going too quickly, lost his footing and slipped; Natalie stopped to help him up. Frightened by the storm, George was heading for the road, out of the camp. The children stood there in the darkness; there was no sign of the man. They needed the lightning to illuminate the zoo once more. Then it came. There he was, there, by the lion wagon, scrabbling with the giant padlocks at the end of the lorry. The children ran towards him. He didn't hear them coming and they dived for his feet, grabbing hold. He yelled and dropped the keys with which he was trying to undo the doors. He lashed out, forced the two children to let him go, prising their small hands off his wet and slippery legs. Then suddenly he was off, running through the zoo. Then there was a shrill blast of a whistle and from the four corners of the zoo ran policemen shining strong torches that captured the shadowy figure in their beam. The man slipped on the wet grass and two policemen launched themselves at him. Landing on the fugitive, they pinned him to the floor. Olaf and Yolanda had reached them. The policemen roughly turned the man over, to get a look at his face. The children didn't believe what they saw. Lying on the ground, writhing and struggling with the bobbies, was one very angry looking man. In the torchlight, they could see who it was – Tom Parker.

Twenty-Five

Mystery Solved

Tom Parker, their friend. He was the face of Templeton's Circus – always a helping hand. A man whom the performers trusted with their lives, as he set about ensuring all their equipment was safe for use each day. It was Tom who would introduce the stars to the paying public; he had always been ready with a joke and a smile.

With ruthless efficiency, the police had removed him to the gaffer's caravan where the children had been allowed to join them. 'They had "saved the show",' said the gaffer; they were entitled to be there at the finish. 'If the lions had got out, it would have been curtains for Templeton's,' he said.

It was crowded in the caravan. The children had never been inside before. The gaffer was a private man. They looked around. The walls were plastered with pictures of the acts that had graced Templeton's ring over the years. Meanwhile, outside, a crowd had gathered, woken by the storm and the shouts that had drifted on the night air. The rain had stopped, the storm having passed. Elsewhere, four circus hands had been dispatched to find George. They had found him eating flowers in a garden nearby. They were lucky; giraffes had been known to badly injure people with a kick from their long legs. He was now safely back in his van.

It was getting light. Tom sat in a chair in the middle of the gaffer's mobile home. He had been handcuffed. He was looking surly, not at all his usual self. *A different man*, thought the children. The fight seemed to have gone out of him. The gaffer looked like he wanted to punch the ringmaster, but a policeman stepped up and the gaffer reluctantly lowered his fists.

Two detectives were facing Tom. 'Have you got anything to say for yourself?' one barked.

Tom had realised that the game was up. He had been caught red-handed. 'I nearly pulled it off,' he declared. 'If it hadn't been for them,' he spat, throwing a black look over his shoulder in the direction of the children. They looked down. The man was suddenly frightening, a threatening presence.

'You'll be wondering why I did it?' said the ringmaster, a dirty smile forming slowly at the side of his mouth. The children realised that he was almost boasting, puffed up with his own importance. He seemed to be enjoying all the attention. He had gone back into "ringmaster mode"; all eyes were upon him – he had "his audience". And, in that moment, the children realised that Tom Parker was a very self-important individual, always wanting to be the centre of everyone's attention.

'Money,' he said. 'It was always about money. Billy Bright offered me £1,000 to put paid to Templeton's. Bright's plan was to come in when Templeton's was on its knees and buy it for a song. I was to be ringmaster with the Bright show next year; their ringmaster is calling it a day. When the gaffer refused to sell, it was down to me to put an end to the tour once and for all, make sure that the jinxed show had no towns that it could visit for the rest of the season. Billy Bright planned to go to those towns with his own show and clean up,' said Tom, with a wry grin.

The gaffer clenched his fists again but the policeman was still there, keeping the two men apart. The children now realised why Bright had gone to see Tom first when he had come to the show. They must have been talking tactics. And, of course Tom had been well placed to bring trouble after trouble the show's way: cut Elena's rope; let Tracy into the cage to attack Chaos; set fire to the elephant tent; poison Josif; sabotage the posters; let Bella loose; and cut the microphone and lights. Now the children came to think about it, the ringmaster had always shown up after each disaster, always been on hand to clean up the mess, take charge after the damage was done – damage he had secretly caused. And of course, he had suggested Gustav and Elena as suspects, to put the children off the scent. It had been his job to have keys to every lock on the show; with them he could get into animals' cages. How clever he had been. *So Bright was in on it all along*, thought the children. They felt pleased with themselves; after all, they had thought he might be involved. But Tom, no, they had never suspected him. Not once.

Dawn was breaking. The detectives led the disgraced ringmaster down the steps and into a waiting police car. Two bobbies had been searching his caravan and had found posters for the Bright show the following season, which featured a big photo of Tom in his ringmaster's costume. The gaffer held one up to the assembled crowd. There were boos and jeers. The circus folk didn't like to be betrayed. They lived together in close harmony. They shared each other's sad times as well as their successes; they were a family. The thought that Tom had been plotting against the show all along turned their stomachs. The policeman placed his hand on the ringmaster's head as he guided him into the back seat.

'But how did the police know to be here tonight?' said Pete.

'Ah,' said the detective, 'not so much of a mystery there. Your teacher, Mr Baker, he phoned us and said he thought something would be planned for the final night; he was worried about you kids; he seems very fond of you.'

The police car drove off slowly over the field. The circus folk were stunned into silence. The gaffer came down the stairs, 'Bacon and eggs for everyone,' he shouted, 'before the pull down.' *The pull down.* The children had forgotten that the circus was moving off that day. Lucy arrived and the children hurriedly told her all that happened. The gaffer came over to where the children stood.

'Look,' he said, 'how can I repay you? If it hadn't been for your quick actions, the lions would have been loose in the town of Torquay; it doesn't bear thinking about. They might even have got hold of poor George and he would have been a gonner. Can you imagine what the papers would have made of all that?'

The children smiled. They were pleased to have helped. Then it hit the school kids. This was goodbye. In a couple of hours, the circus children would be gone. The school kids felt their tummies lurch; Lucy took a big gulp; even Pete forced back a tear.

'Listen,' said the gaffer. 'There's two weeks of the school holidays left, so I've heard. Why don't you spend it with us, come on tour for the next two weeks?'

The school kids looked at one another. Could they? Would their parents agree?

'Maybe this Mr Baker would talk to your parents, reassure them that we circus folk can we trusted,' suggested the gaffer, 'square it with them. You're heroes, you are, together with our own kids, of course.'

The school children blushed. They didn't like such talk. They had only been trying to help. Anyone would have done the same.

Their friend, Mr Baker, did speak to their parents and they each agreed to let the children go off for the last two weeks of the holidays; even Lucy's parents were persuaded. Parents hurriedly packed suitcases for them as the show aimed to be off the ground by midday. Lucy was to stay with Natalie and Yolanda; Pete with Timmy and Olaf; Clive and Annie with Laurent's parents.

The friends' parents drove them to the ground. The tent was already down and loaded on to its truck. Some of the wagons had already left. The four friends were allocated to a particular lorry or van. Pete was in the last lorry to leave the field. He leant out of the window and stared at the now empty field. It was hard to imagine that this had been home to so much action. It was once again a plain field, empty and forlorn. Meanwhile, they were heading for Plymouth. This was truly unexpected. A big coastal town, where they would stay for just a week, and then they would go onto Weymouth. At both towns, children were already looking at posters that announced Templeton's Circus was coming.

Billy Bright was arrested and confessed to his part in the scheme. His show then promptly folded. What Mr Baker would have called ironic, chimed the school children, laughing.

The school kids had the time of their lives over the next two weeks. Pete and Clive were invited to help with the cats; Gustav and Isabella were intent on mixing their two acts. The gaffer had persuaded the Slovakians to stay with Templeton's next season. A combined act of tigers and lions would be the star attraction. It would be hard work that was for sure. The different cats were naturally suspicious of one another. Getting them used to a new routine would take patience.

Annie and Lucy got to help with the elephants, even riding them when the gaffer wasn't around. Elena returned to the show. It was unlikely that she would ever perform in the air again; her wrists had been too badly damaged. The gaffer offered to buy her an act with "poodles" that she could learn to show. It was something; not what she would have wanted, but there it was. She had Pieter and circus folk had to be flexible.

The show had always to go on! There were walks to the sea and eating outside. The children slept outside too. Pete and Natalie joined forces and persuaded Manu to give the elephants an outdoor area, a first for a UK circus, and Isabella persuaded Gustav to persevere with an exercise run for their cats. Templeton's circus was changing, just a little – new people had brought new ideas.

Templeton's had a replacement ringmaster, Jimmy Jones. A man who was as short as Tom Parker was tall. Like the previous ringmaster, he was full of smiles but the circus folk opted to put their trust in him. There couldn't be two men like Tom Parker – no show could be that unlucky!

There were still cranks outside each show in Plymouth and Bournemouth. There was no Dave character, but he was replaced easily by new faces who stepped forward. The circus children ignored them. Only Natalie and Pete continued to sympathise with the protesters. But there was no point falling out. Animals were still part of the show. The day might come when they were not, but that looked to be some way off: the crowds kept on coming and the gaffer was a strong believer in giving the punters what they wanted.

At the end of the two weeks, the time came for the children to bid their farewells. Their parents had driven to collect them. It was time for school on Monday. The boys slapped each other on the back and the girls hugged. Natalie gave Pete a final kiss goodbye. And then they were off; the school kids all glancing back, watching their waving circus friends standing at the gate. It seemed weird. Was it really all over?

The circus friends turned round to walk back to the show. They would approach school differently in the future. Maybe it didn't always have to be a case of them and us. They wouldn't meet four friends like Pete, Clive, Annie and Lucy again, but there might be other friendly faces, children who would be prepared to include them.

The next day, Monday, saw the four school friends kitted out in their new uniforms. Crisp shirts and blouses, neatly pressed; grey trousers and skirts; shiny black shoes, so shiny you could see your faces in them. Big school! They were nervous. What would they be asked to do on the first day? They congregated in the playground before the bell, along with two hundred other children for whom it was also the start of a new adventure. The corridors were busy places, full of bigger kids, but somehow they felt more confident after their summer of adventures. They made their way into their new class. They were to be altogether. It was a relief; they hadn't wanted to be separated. They sat down in class and the teacher strode in.

'Right,' she said with a smile. 'Let's think back to the holidays,' and walking to the board, she wrote: *What I did this summer*. Pete, Lucy, Clive and Annie smiled at one another. Where should they begin?

Epilogue

He wandered back to their caravan. She was there, taking off her makeup, winding down after flying high.

'Natalie,' he said quietly. 'I've been thinking back to that summer in Torquay, the summer of '75. Do you remember it?'

'I wondered where you were,' she smiled. 'I'd like to know what all those kids are doing now,' she said. 'I was quite fond of that Pete.'

He laughed. 'Don't try and make me jealous.'

'Jealous,' she said. 'I chose you, didn't I? Funny though,' she added, 'how things turned out. Both Pete and I were against the use of wild animals in the show and now they're all gone! Banned! The cranks had their way in the end. But, we do okay without them. The show goes on...'

'What about Tom Parker?' said Laurent. 'I wonder whatever became of him?'

'Laurent,' she whispered, 'pass me the photo album, will you, darling?'

He passed the collection to his wife. 'There we are,' she said, running her hand slowly over a faded photo. It was the picture of the circus performers making a human pyramid, with their school friends from that summer standing in front. 'What a time that was,' she said. 'I can remember it like it was yesterday.'

'Hmmn,' he murmured. 'Maybe we should take our show to Torquay this summer, look them up. I wonder if Pete ever became a doctor. It would be fun to find out what they're all up to now.'

It was an idea. One they liked, very much: Torquay in the summer – it sounded like fun, a real adventure!